THE ITINERANT LODGER

David Nobbs was born in Orpington and educated at Marlborough, Cambridge and in the Royal Corps of Signals. His first job was as a reporter on the *Sheffield Star*, and his first break as a comedy writer came on the iconic satire show *That Was The Week, That Was*, hosted by David Frost. Later he wrote for *The Frost Report* and *The Two Ronnies* and provided material for many top comedians including Les Dawson, Ken Dodd, Tommy Cooper, Frankie Howerd and Dick Emery. David is best known for his two TV hit series *A Bit of a Do* and for *The Fall and Rise of Reginald Perrin*, now revived in a contemporary version, starring Martin Clunes. He lives in North Yorkshire with his second wife, Susan. He has four stepchildren, eight grand-stepchildren and one great-grand-stepchild.

Praise for David Nobbs's novels:

'Painfully hilarious, wonderfully observed and slight sour at the same time'   *Guardian*

'Thank goodness for David Nobbs! He carries on the comic tradition of P G Wodehouse with this marvellous new book; a sweet and touching love story written with his trademark sly and subversive humour. A perfect antidote to these dark times'   JOANNE HARRIS

'Probably our finest post-war comic novelist'   JONATHAN COE

'A marvellously comic novel'   *Sunday Times*

'One of the most noisily funny books I have ever read'   MICHAEL PALIN

'Very funny sketches of provincial newspaper life'   SUE TOWNSEND

'The most satisfying novel I have read in years'   *Express*

Also by David Nobbs

Obstacles to Young Love
A Piece of the Sky is Missing
Ostrich Country

DAVID NOBBS

The Itinerant Lodger

HARPER

Harper
An imprint of HarperCollins*Publishers*
77–85 Fulham Palace Road,
Hammersmith, London W6 8JB

www.harpercollins.co.uk

This paperback edition 2010

First published in Great Britain by
Methuen & Co Ltd 1965

A catalogue record for this book is
available from the British Library

ISBN: 978 0 00 742788 8

Typeset in Garamond by Palimpsest Book Production Limited,
Falkirk, Stirlingshire

Find out more about HarperCollins and the environment at
www.harpercollins.co.uk/green

I

A FEELING OF NERVOUS EXCITEMENT CREPT SHYLY over Wilson, and he rubbed his hands together. Here he was, at this very moment in time and space, old Wilson himself, standing in a bus queue in this exciting great city, waiting to be swept off to his new destination – 38, Trebisall Avenue. Here he was, at last, after all these wasted years. It seemed too good to be true, and he took the letter from his pocket and read it for the third time, to make sure.

"Dear Mr Box 221/F2" it ran. "Having regard to your advertisement of third inst. late night final, I am pleased to be able to inform you that I am in possession of accommodation just such as you require. It is a nice, spacious bed-sitting room, affording a pleasant vista over my cosy little garden, with use of same. Heating is by gas fire and the furnishings are tasteful. All meals are provided, and I know how to cater for men. You will find no unnecessary restrictions here and will be very happy. If your arrival should be by train, the 91 bus leaves straight opposite (East exit). Ask for Pantons, and I am on left. The charge of four pounds per week is inclusive of meals, laundry and lighting – but not heat – and I hope to hear that this is to your satisfaction. I remain Mrs Pollard, etc."

Yes, it was to his satisfaction all right, he thought, putting the letter back in his pocket. There would be peace and quiet here. Here he would be able to work, overlooking the garden. Already he felt certain that this city would provide the inspiration that had been lacking. Here at last was the land of opportunity, the new land in which it would be possible for him to discover the universal panacea for all mankind.

He had come far that day, over the hills. Already it was late

5

afternoon, and there still remained the bus ride. Dusk would be falling – dusk, that exciting, nerve-racking season of the day – as he was shown into that vacant room where his life's work was to begin. He picked up his suitcase impatiently, hoping to encourage the bus company by his example. It was all he had brought, that suitcase, and it contained everything that was his in the world. It was a case of medium size, with a floral lining. A plastic bag, joined to the inside of the case by buttons, served as a container for his washing things. It was a fine case, and he had packed it with a determined attempt at neatness, although there was nothing neat about the way in which the pyjamas were wrapped round the railway sandwich that he had not eaten, or about the green stains which were smeared over the book that he had not read. His toothpaste had fallen from the plastic bag during the journey, and there were green stains too upon his shirts, his three shirts, and upon the quarto sheets, on which as yet there were no poems.

At last the 91 arrived. He sat in the front seat upstairs, in order not to miss Pantons when it came, and also because he always did sit in the front seat upstairs, if it was empty. If there was so much as one person seated there he gave it a wide berth, but if it was empty he sat there, and it was empty now.

The streets were enclosed in the light from shop fronts and warmed by the bustle of the crowds as the gloom and mist of late afternoon thickened. On the left the land fell away towards the river and the canal, and beyond the river, beside the railway, the slender chimneys of the factories could still be seen against the fading sky. From time to time a molten splash of flame would roar from a chimney and send sparks of drama far over the valley. Wilson liked this, and he liked also the land on the right, where grimy cul-de-sacs lined the steep slopes of the hill, and the snow was edged by globules of soot. Above the streets rose the flinty, messy summit of the hill, scarred by open-cast mining and pocked with sunken air-raid shelters, as though the city had gone bald from shock. Wilson was becoming increasingly nervous, as he had known he would, and although he noted all this precisely it made no conscious impression on him.

Soon the moment of arrival would come. It was useless to tell himself that he was merely arriving at lodgings – and unknown lodgings at that. He was arriving at the beginning of life itself, and the dryness of his throat grew feverishly tight. He wished that the dusk could enfold him and the cheerful crowds could swallow him up.

He sat rigidly in his seat, wanting and ceasing to want, not wanting and ceasing not to want. Pantons was alongside before he noticed it, and by the time he had struggled to the top of the stairs, where the nearest bell was situated, the bus had carried him past Trebisall Avenue, past Ashton Road, and, did he but know it, almost to Tuffley Corner.

It was much colder in these residential streets, but despite the cold Wilson walked slowly through the fading light. Soon, all too soon, he found Trebisall Avenue. Somewhere up there was number 38, and somewhere in number 38 was Mrs Pollard, who had answered his advertisement. She had Italic handwriting.

He paused at the door of number 38, delaying his knock. He was near to panic now. Then, without being aware of it, he had knocked. There was the sound of slow footsteps, and heavy breathing. A face flattened itself against the frosted glass, and the door was slowly opened. Mrs Pollard stood before him.

"You'll be Mr Barnes," she said.

2

THE HOUSE WAS FILLED WITH THE AURA OF IMPENDING stew. Mrs Pollard led Barnes to his room and pointed out the sofa which it would be his task to convert into a bed each night.

"I hope you'll be comfortable," she said. "It makes all the difference when you're away from home, whether you're comfortable. Not that there'll be any need for you to feel away from home in this house. There's an hour left in the fire, so you'll be all right for a bit."

"Thank you, Mrs Pollard."

"You'll be hungry after your long journey. I've a meal on for you. Stew."

"Thank you. That'll be nice."

"Yes. You'd as well to let me know if you don't like it. Not that I approve of fads, but there it is, if you don't like it you'd as well to let me know. We're very partial to stews in this house."

"We?"

"The old man upstairs. Not that he eats."

There was a brief silence. Then, uneasily, Mrs Pollard asked him: "Will you take your dinner in with me, Mr Barnes, or would you rather have it in here?"

"In here would be very nice, thank you," he replied, glancing mechanically round the room.

"As you wish," she said, and she closed the door behind her.

Barnes lit the fire with one of his seven remaining matches. Then suddenly he felt that a spell of breathing was about to assail him. He lay back on the sofa, in the manner that he had found most suitable, and awaited it. Quite soon it came. Wave after wave of breathing flooded him, and sent all his thoughts to his brain, where they jostled for the best positions. It was useless to attempt to pick any of them out. There was nothing for it but to lie there and wait for them to stop.

Soon it was all over, and he went to the window. It was dark, and the lights of the houses were patterned all over the hills. His thoughts were settling down now, and as he stood there, gazing into the darkness, he thought of his life to date. An education, that was all it had been. Cambridge and Winchester. Fine names. The Pay Corps. A fine regiment. And then, after Cambridge, the hard school of life. A brief spell on the newspaper, serving the interests of Droitwich and its environs. A short while detecting earthquakes. A stint in the kitchens, specialising in savouries and nougat. A variety of little jobs, of odds and ends of one kind and another, all performed with varying degrees of utter incompetence.

8

It had all been nothing but a preparation. Now, in this great city, Barnes, thirty-nine, of no fixed abode, would discover the purpose of existence. Here, in this bed-sitting room, the humiliations and trials of the past would serve their purpose. He knew it. Already much of his nervousness had passed away, for the arrival had been smoother than he had dared to hope.

He was still by the window when Mrs Pollard returned with the silver casserole – a prize for lupins. Proudly she placed it on the table, and then she removed the lid, with its valued inscription in the best Latin that money could buy.

"I've brought you your dinner," she said, and he came over from the window and took his position behind it. He felt suddenly hungry, and he ate, as always, with frenzied, uncritical zeal. He was well liked wherever he ate. Mrs Pollard sat opposite, presiding over him intently, and the long, heavy silence was broken only by the steady munch of his eating. As the meal drew to a close, and the eating ceased to occupy all his attention, he began to wish that she was not in the room with him. He felt that it was not the done thing, in the early stages of a landlady-lodger relationship, and he felt doubly glad that he had not chosen to eat in her room.

His nervousness had returned, and he felt a shock when Mrs Pollard asked him how he had found the stew.

"Very good," he said hastily.

"Say if it's not," she said. "We may as well get things straight from the start."

"No," he assured her. "I meant it."

Silence fell again, heavier even than before. This time there was no eating to disturb it, and at length, with a great effort, Mrs Pollard spoke.

"Would you like some coffee?" she inquired. "Or some tea?"

"Coffee would be very nice, thank you."

"I'll fetch you some coffee."

Over coffee they talked a little.

"You're familiar with these parts?" she asked.

"I've not been here before, no."

9

"We were new to it too."

"We?"

"Pollard. He was Birmingham and I'm Hornchurch."

Why didn't she go, now, back to Hornchurch, or at least to her kitchen, where a landlady belongs? He longed for her to go.

"What part do you come from?" she asked at length.

"London and Margate and Evesham and Barnstaple and the Isle of Wight."

"Well, I never. And it's the Isle of Wight you've come from now, is it? Quite a change for you, this must be."

"No. I've come from Birmingham."

"Oh. Like Pollard." There was another pause, broken once more by Mrs Pollard. "You had a good job in Birmingham, I suppose?"

"I was a teacher."

"Oh. Very nice."

"I taught scripture and games."

"And now you're going to be a teacher here too."

"No. No, I'm starting afresh. I'm going to be a writer."

"Oh. Very nice. What sort of thing will you write, if it isn't a rude question?"

It wasn't a rude question, and so he felt that he ought to reply. "Poems," he said, somewhat surlily.

"A poem is a lovely thing."

"Yes."

An impasse! Mrs Pollard made no attempt to get round it. She sensed that further inquiries might not be welcome yet, and for this he was grateful. He was also grateful to her for making no reference to the rent.

"I'll go and put the kettle on for your bottle," she said. "You want to feel well-aired after a long journey."

While she was gone Barnes fetched from his suitcase a sheet of blank quarto writing paper. On it he wrote: "Poem, by Barnes," and then he placed it in the middle of his table, where it would await him in the morning.

"I'll show you how to make your bed," Mrs Pollard said on her return, and he followed her to the sofa. She lifted the back of the sofa to its full extent, and then she brought the seat forward and at the same time lowered it, to reveal, where previously there had been only a sofa, a bed. She then pursued the reverse process, taking care to lift the under-bar so that the springs wouldn't catch and be torn to ribbons. She then asked Barnes to demonstrate, just for her peace of mind. He proved a most unresponsive pupil, and it was several minutes before she felt that she could safely leave him. To him these minutes were as charged with the torture of practical anguish as those dreadful hours that he had spent making and remaking his bed pack, in the Pay Corps, long ago, during his formative years. He was in no doubt, at moments like these – and there were many such – that one of the primary causes of his arrested development had been the diversity and complexity of the sleeping arrangements that he had been required to master. There was a certain hammock, in particular, that he would never quite forget.

"Well," said Mrs Pollard at last, "there it is. That's the best I can do for you."

"Thank you."

"It's not a bad bed, really. Pollard won it in a newspaper. He arranged ten hardy annuals in the order in which he would like to be given them for Christmas. We used to sleep in it. I suppose it has a sentimental value for me. It's really quite a good bed. Big, too. Big enough for two, wouldn't you say?"

But Barnes did not tell her what he would have said. He was polite enough to wait until she had returned with his stone hot water bottle, and then, when she had finally left the room, he fainted.

3

THE MORNING WAS CRISP AND WHITE, IDEAL FOR shaving. Barnes had slept well, as he always did after fainting, and as he shaved he felt in excellent form. The quarto sheets were waiting for him, the water was hot, and soon his work would begin. He could hear Mrs Pollard going about her morning tasks in another part of the house, and for a moment he felt uneasy. He hoped that she wasn't going to make demands on him. Then he dismissed the thought and turned to more important things.

When he had shaved he dressed and when he had dressed he raised the main part of his bed and slid it back towards the head, to reveal, where previously there had been only a bed, a sofa. Then Mrs Pollard brought him his breakfast. She asked him how he was, how he had slept, what were his plans, but they had little conversation, and he hardly minded her presence. He ate fast, for he was intoxicated by the infinite possibilities that were whirring about in his head. He had never before felt as strong as he did at this moment.

At last the breakfast things were cleared, and he was alone. He seated himself at the table and gazed proudly round the room. There was the sofa, the piano, the table, the easy chair and the hard chair. He noted with delight the Scottish glen above the piano, the Dresden hyenas on the mantelpiece, the tapestried axioms above the sofa, the two ivory ospreys, between which there were as yet no books, and the old polished range in the middle of which, like a neon cat, his absurdly small gas fire sat hissing. During the night there had been virtually no vacant floor space even to put his shoes and socks in, and even now, when the bed had become a sofa, the room was small. And although there was a window behind the sofa, affording a pleasant vista over Mrs Pollard's cosy little garden, it afforded very little light, the cosiness being caused by high walls and surrounding houses. Yet despite all this he looked around him with joy. Here was the haven that he had sought, in which he could distil the experience of a long and lonely life. Here was something that was his, and yet did not belong to him, and would not clutter him up.

The sheet of quarto writing paper lay on the table where he had left it. Beside it was his HB pencil, and beside the pencil lay his souvenir rubber, on which the letters "ME TO MA" suggested a filial devotion that circumstance had, in fact, denied him. Originally the rubber had read "WELCOME TO MARGATE."

He picked up his pencil. It was a moment to savour, and he was still savouring it an hour and a half later when Mrs Pollard brought him his coffee. Then, after his coffee, he began to write.

For the next ten days he sat at the table, free. He ate egg and bacon for breakfast, stews for lunch and cold meats for supper, and between meals he wrote. Every now and then he would add a word to the collection that he was gathering in front of him, and every now and then he would discard a sheet of paper into the waste paper basket. Every now and then Mrs Pollard would take the waste paper basket to the dustbin, and twice a week the dustman, who had no knowledge of poetry, would empty the bin into a lorry. So there was no chance of the dustman bursting in and exclaiming: "I can't accept this. It isn't rubbish. It's a masterpiece." No, once it was gone it was gone. And each time he arrived at the end of a sheet it was gone, gone for ever. For nothing that he wrote seemed good enough to keep.

Often he would sit for many minutes without writing. It was not so much that he could not think of a word. That, with the dictionary to help him, presented no problem. It was rather that he found it impossible to decide which word to choose, of all those that were available to him in such abundance. His hopes were so high, his possibilities so infinite, that each actual word crushed him with its puniness. The moment a word was conveyed to paper, it seemed ridiculous. Why, he would ask himself, should he start with that? Or finish with it, for that matter? So that he was for ever adding words at both ends, until the original word had become lost in a welter of qualifications and preambles, and had to be discarded. And once it was discarded the whole structure around it collapsed, and it was necessary to begin again.

But how? He tried several methods. He tried selecting at random the first word of each line, and then working forwards, or selecting the last word, and working backwards. He tried writing the first word of the first line, the second word of the second line, the third word of the third line, and so on, and then going back and filling in the gaps, just as he had done with his impots at prep school. He tried writing down words which he knew to be conducive of poetic inspiration, words like "spring" and "autumn" and "corpses" and "e'er" and "o'er". All to no avail. As those ten long days passed, the moments when he wrote no words grew longer, and longer, and longer.

And all the while Mrs Pollard was finding excuses to visit his room. She would leave things there and have to return for them. She would think she heard the shilling finish in his fire. She would bring him a cup of tea and an assortment of sweet biscuits. Each time she came she seemed to hover over him, and each time, had there been a train to his thought, she would have broken it.

Finally, towards dusk on the tenth day, when he had not added a word for many hours, she remarked: "Still working, then?"

"Er, yes." He was annoyed at the interruption, although it interrupted nothing.

"You'll get round shoulders. Still, it's none of my business."

"No."

"I've never really been creative myself." She had taken the fact that he had replied as an invitation, and had seated herself on the sofa, setting off a series of twangings and screechings that irritated Barnes beyond measure. "I've never really had anything to say," she continued. "But you. . . ." she paused, and for the first time for ten days Barnes looked at her as if she existed.

"I?"

"You have something to say."

"And how am I going to say it?"

14

"In your poems."

"I've written no poems."

"You said you were writing poems. I was led to believe that you were writing poems. I don't expect my tenants to lock themselves away for days on end, not speaking to me, and not even a couplet to show for it."

"I tried."

With astonishing speed a soft maternity enveloped Mrs Pollard. "You're new to this business, aren't you?" she asked.

He blushed and fidgeted awkwardly. "Yes," he admitted.

"You aren't really a poet at all."

"No."

"As if I minded. You could have told me."

"I didn't know."

"No offence, I hope. Some of my best friends haven't been poets. But I said to myself when you mentioned it: 'That one a poet? H'm. I wonder.'"

Barnes replied quite mechanically to her maternity. All the verse had gone out of him. Of infinite possibilities he no longer had the slightest inkling. He was a boy again, and he could think of nothing to say to this new mother of his.

"Perhaps you'll think of something later on," said Mrs Pollard. "Some blank verse, or a nice hexameter. There's no harm in keeping on trying."

"I'm just not a poet."

"You mustn't say things like that. Faint heart never won fair lady."

His faint heart fluttered like a moth with thrombosis, and he lowered his eyes.

"I'll make you a stew," she said, as if it was a thought that had just occurred to her for the first time and had opened up visions far in excess of those she had ever imagined. "Perhaps that'll cheer you up."

"Thank you."

"You do like my stews, don't you? You aren't tired of them?"

"Not at all, no."

15

"You aren't just saying that?"

"No, I – it would be very nice."

Left to himself, he made a final great effort to concentrate on his work. It was no use giving up. What would Chaucer's friends have said if he'd packed the whole thing up just before Strood? The possibilities were even more infinite than he had imagined. Well, he must be that much more determined. It was a challenge, and he must rise to it. Perhaps he had been trying in the wrong way. Perhaps there had been something over-deliberate in his approach. Well, he must try a more open method, make himself more receptive, allow his thoughts and images freedom to form in their own good time. He decided to make his mind go a complete blank. This it did instantly, and it was still a complete blank when Mrs Pollard returned.

"I wondered if you'd like a little garlic?" she inquired coyly.

"Yes, that would be very nice."

"Only some do and some don't."

Garlic. No garlic. Could she really think he cared?

"You've done nothing yet, then?"

"Not yet."

"Never mind. Keep trying. It's a fine thing, poetry. It's not anything about the house, is it?"

"What do you mean?"

"It's not because you're not happy here?"

"Oh no. No."

"I hope you'll be happy. Mr Veal has never complained."

"Mr Veal?"

"The old man upstairs."

"Oh."

"With garlic, then."

He resumed his creative activities. Nothing happened. The possibilities became so infinite, and the infinite stretched so far, that it seemed as if it might burst into a million fragments. Instead it receded. Far into the distance, with infinite slowness, it slid. He had no power to follow it, and a flat despair came upon him. For a while he was aware of nothing at all, but then odours of stew began to impinge themselves on his misery. He realised that he was hungry.

The odours came from the kitchen, and were constantly changing in the strangest ways. Where was Mrs Pollard? Why did she not bring him his stew? A simple comfort would have been most welcome. He had had comforts in his time. Miss Potter, Mrs McManus of Barnstaple, Mrs Egham, Mrs McManus of Newport (I.O.W.) and Mrs Bell, they all had seen to that. And now there was Mrs Pollard. She was mothering him, and trying to make him happy in a thousand little ways. Her hair was growing white, and she wanted to make him happy. And yet he wondered. What lay behind it? Maternal instincts he had seen, but were there others? He waited and waited, and his uneasiness grew.

4

NOT SINCE MR JENNINGS HAD MRS POLLARD FELT SO much concern over a stew. She wanted to make Barnes a stew that he would never forget, a stew that would help him to overcome his worries and inspire him to write his poems. She opened the door of the fridge and gazed at the frosted wonderland inside. She went to the cupboard and peered at the rows of smiling edibles that stood in its dark, spicy depths. And she realised that for the first time in her life she was at a loss where to begin.

In desperation she consulted Thorneycroft's *Thought For Food* and started to read Chapter One: "Your Guest Arrives". She had never before sought the advice of the great culinary philosopher and gastrophile, but then she had never before been at a loss. In the past her stews had just happened. One minute they had not been there and the next minute, hey presto, there they had been.

The most important thing to consider, in choosing a menu, was the nature of the person who would eat the food. However carefully prepared, however exquisitely cooked, however delight-fully presented a meal might be, it could not be a complete suc-cess unless it was served to the right person, said Thorneycroft, and Mrs Pollard believed him. But although he gave examples of kinds of people – the ascetic scholar was one, and the young executive was another – none of them were remotely like Barnes. What kind of a person could he possibly be? She turned to the chapter on stews, but to no purpose. Each recipe was absolutely delicious, of that she had no doubt, but which of them was right for her Barnsey?

In the end she had to abandon the book – a Christmas present – and return to her shelves. But it was no use. She was quite in-capable of deciding which ingredients to use, and eventually, with a sudden despairing decision she relinquished control of her faculties and flung into the casserole the first objects that came to hand – some capers, an onion, some stewing beef, a sprig of tarra-gon, a lobster, some plums, and a sheet of gelatine. Onto all that she poured some stock.

While these ingredients were settling down she went to Barnes' room and asked him about the garlic, and then, after she had returned and added the garlic, she tasted the stew. It was dis-pleasing. She fetched from the larder a bay leaf, some more stew-ing beef, a bottle of sherry, another onion, and some carrots. She put a spoonful of sherry and the carrots into the stew, tasted it again, and grimaced. It still displeased her, though not so strongly as before.

At first she was not unhappy. She was performing a heroic holding action, and it occupied all her energies. But when she had tried every imaginable combination of ingredients, and the stew had still not become more than a pathetic shadow of the feast on which she had set her heart, she grew very depressed. She went to see Veal, as was her custom when things became too much for her.

She climbed slowly the dark, narrow, creaking staircase. She was panting and having great difficulty in breathing and before she entered his room she waited for it to die down.

Veal was asleep, and Mrs Pollard sat quietly for a few minutes on a wooden chair at the side of his bed. Then, when she felt calmer, she adjusted his sheets and tidied the bottom of his bed, making sure that the blankets were properly tucked in. She brushed his shoes, wound up his alarm clock, made certain that his suitcases were arranged in inverse order of size, and then stood at the bottom of the bed and looked down on him where he slept. She stood there for a few moments, and then she realised with a shock that she had been thinking of other things – of Barnes, of the stew, and of how she could make things easier for him in a thousand little ways.

She hastened downstairs and began once more to taste the stew. She did so with horror. She had hoped that in the interim it might have matured, or that, returning to it after a breather, she would find that her fears had been exaggerated. But it seemed, if anything, even less tasty than before. It was very far from being the ideal stew after which she had hankered.

She realised now, when it was too late, that the success of a stew depends not so much on the nature of the ingredients as upon their relationships among themselves, one to another. The sweetest carrot tastes bitter inside a camembert. At first the introduction of ingredients into the casserole had improved the stew, but only at first. She had introduced too many, far too many, so that it had become a struggle for survival down there in the cauldron. It would be difficult to state the exact moment at which the stew had ceased to improve, and had begun to deteriorate. Very likely it was with the introduction of the lobster. Anyway Mrs Pollard became certain that, could she but remove the lobster, the dish would become, if not ideal, at least edible. The lobster, however, had disintegrated, as lobsters will, given the slightest encouragement, and had permeated the stew to such an extent that not only was there nothing which could be said to be the lobster, but there was nothing that could be said not to be.

The only thing for it was to remove from the wreckage those objects which she judged most likely to be completely distasteful, and which were still sufficiently whole to be distinguishable –

the sprig of tarragon, for instance. After removing each object she tasted the remainder and to her delighted surprise it began to grow more and more edible. With increasing excitement she removed objects and with increasing relish she tasted what was left. Really, it was almost delicious. She removed something which looked suspiciously like a burnt carrot, and ate another spoonful. She decided that it was perfect. At last! She had done it, and she could have cried for joy.

It was at this moment that she discovered that not a morsel of stew remained. She had just eaten the last spoonful.

5

FOR A FEW MOMENTS HER HAND QUIVERED ON THE knob of his door, but she exerted no pressure, and the handle did not turn. Her stomach felt hollow. Her hands were weak. Once or twice she wavered, as if she was plucking up her courage and determining to walk boldly into his room and tell him the terrible news, but in reality she already knew that she would not.

She walked slowly through the kitchen, past the dying fire and the deserted knitting basket, and crept up the narrow staircase. Up there, separated from Veal by a thin and peeling wall, she lay wakeful. In the distance a steel bar was being hammered upon her forehead, and nearer at hand, a long while later, she heard a jangled squeak, as Barnes converted his sofa into a bed.

For he had noticed suddenly that the fire had gone out. He stood up, stretched painfully, and creaked into the kitchen. All round the range stood pots and pans and tins, and there, in the centre, was the empty, unwashed casserole. It was most strange.

Hunger was biting into him, and furtively he found some bread and ate three slices, dry. After that there was no point in staying up, so he cleaned his teeth, undressed, placed his clothes untidily over the back of his wooden chair, tightened the cord of his pyjamas, converted his sofa into a bed, and crept into it. The moon rose in a sky that was cold and hard and empty at last of snow. The trees drooped under the weight of the snow that had fallen, and there was no movement anywhere. He drifted towards sleep without reaching it, and he settled down for a long vigil, gazing at the ceiling till his eyes smarted, remembering the nights when it had thundered and he had longed to lie warm and crumpled beside whatever mother he had at the time. In this way he came near to the warmth of sleep, and then suddenly he was awake again, and there it was inside him, happiness. It forced him out of bed and sent him scampering to the window.

The moon was falling over the bare top of a hill, and light fingers of cloud were stretching wakefully across the sky. A grey light was beginning to spread from the east, and from the earth a thin steam was rising and dying as it rose. Mists began to gather and the sky turned slowly orange. Here and there a bird sang in surprise at finding itself alive on such a morning, after the storm.

The morning! In the morning he would start to discover the purpose of existence. It was not here, in this dingy room. It was not inside himself. It was not to be found through the rarefied isolation of artistic creation, even if what he had produced had been art. He realised that now. It was out there on the sides of the hills, where people lived, and in the factories, where they worked. He must work, feel himself useful, and embark upon a voyage of discovery. In the morning he would find himself a job. In the morning he would thrill to the vibrant excitement of human activity. In the morning he would become a new man, Fletcher.

Meanwhile he closed the curtain and went back to bed, and fell, like Mrs Pollard, into a kind of sleep.

6

FLETCHER EMERGED THREE HOURS LATER IN A MANNER
that astounded Mrs Pollard. His face, taking cheerfulness almost
to the point of no return, carried all before it in a manner that
she had not seen from him before. In her embarrassment she
assumed that he would mention the events of the previous evening, but he made no reference to them. Rather he announced his
intention of taking a short walk before breakfast. This could have
knocked Mrs Pollard over with a feather. Judge then of her
shock when she saw him leap down the steps in one bound and
set off in the general direction of the Midland Station at a pro-
nounced trot, rubbing his hands eagerly together.

She couldn't understand it, and she didn't like it. He had never
taken a walk at any time, let alone before breakfast, and he had
certainly never rubbed his hands together when she was looking.
However, there was no time to worry about that. She must make
him his breakfast. Stew.

It was not the usual thing for breakfast, but she felt that there
would be no peace between them until she had redeemed herself.
She decided, having learnt from her mistake, to aim at something simple, and she chose from her larder onions, potatoes,
carrots, stewing beef and haricot beans. Onto these she poured a
generous proportion of stock. Next she secured to the floor, at a
yard's distance from the casserole, a wooden chair, and she then
sat on it. She began to stir the stew. This she did with an enormous spoon. It really was enormous, for a spoon. One would have
been excused had one mistaken it for a dredging bucket. This
spoon, this great spoon, had once belonged to Builth Evans, of
the Merioneth Axe Murders, and had become a valuable family
heirloom. Mrs Pollard, who was descended from the Evanses on
her grandmother's side, was extremely proud of the spoon, and

22

had made a will bequeathing it to the Victoria and Albert Museum in London, should it survive her. It was over four feet long and had at its head a curious double joint, characteristic of the best Welsh domestic spoons. The purpose of this joint was to allow the spoon to lie in the vertical while the handle was in the horizontal position, and vice versa. When the handle of the spoon was wiggled, the wiggle communicated itself, via the joint, to the spoon, thus setting up a cross-wiggle. The result was a stir only slightly inferior to that obtainable with any other spoon.

Mrs Pollard believed that by thus employing the spoon she was making it useful, and that it was therefore a boon to her, in that it was of use. Wearisome and clumsy though her efforts were, she firmly believed that she was using a labour-saving device.

Fletcher, in the meantime, was advancing by leaps and bounds, as he grappled with the problems involved in discovering a new city. His nervous excitement led him on a prodigious walk, up and down the hills, through parks, past quaint old pubs and great modern stores, the dreams of master hacks. On all sides stretched streets of square brick houses, appealing or appalling, according to one's spelling. Eventually, at the end of one of these streets, he came upon a vista. Below him lay the valley and the factories, and on the other side of the valley a belt of derelict open spaces and car parks threaded its way into the centre of the city and petered out among a mass of printing presses, garages and canteen windows. Beyond them, on the right, rose the towers and spires of the principal buildings.

Fletcher stopped walking and leant against the wall, looking out over this new land. The city was given over, in the main, to heavy industry. A hundred years ago, he mused, it had been little more than a collection of villages, each with its own peculiar customs and institutions. Now it housed, he estimated, some half a million souls, several of them taxi-drivers, others lawyers, journalists, smelters and so on, down through the whole gamut of human activity. There was not much here, he judged, to attract the tourist, but there was a thriving air of activity which would no doubt compensate for the lack of historical interest and beauty. The inhabitants, he felt sure, retained the traditions of independence and individuality which their manly life had given their forefathers.

It was to be his domain! In this great city lay his life's work. He strode on, past the Salvation Dining Rooms, the Midland Station, the Hippodrome Cinema, the *Telegraph and Chronicle* Building and the Temperance Launderette. He passed the imposing façade of the Neo-Gothic Town Hall, on whose well-kept lawns summer time crowds enjoyed, in *son et lumière*, the dramatised history of the Chamber of Commerce. He passed the sandstone and soot cathedral and the Northern Productivity Pavilion, and the whole bustle of the early-morning life of the city fired his imagination. He drank in the atmosphere as if he could not have enough of it. It was a beautiful morning. Quite soon it would snow, but at this moment the sun, high above the slate roofs, was shining on the upturned faces of the buses. The city was full of noise. The market was situated on the hill. The politicians were driven in the big, black cars. The pencil was in the pocket of the publican. The tourist was purchasing a tin of luncheon meat. The street trader was displaying many kinds of produce. The townsfolk were travelling to work. See, the merchant has raised his glass and is drinking. Why, the newsvendor is selling those journals with ease.

So the city went about its business, and Fletcher watched. This was the promised land, and it seemed natural that a military ceremony should take place and martial music should sweep him into battle. He was not certain of the purpose of the parade, nor did he know the identity of the elderly lady who stood in the uniform of a field marshal on the dais, but he stood near her and watched the troops march past. Contingent after contingent swept by in perfect step. The sun shone on the green berets of the Third Battalion the Queen's Own Mexborough Fusiliers and glinted off the campaign medals on the chests of the Old Comrades and the veterans of Ladysmith. There was cheering from the crowds as the military bands played and swept Fletcher towards his duty.

There was so much that must be saved. As he marched he saw the world waiting to be saved. Africa, Asia, America, Europe. Mountains, rivers and forests. Rivers running through the forests. Mountains emerging out of the forests. Fletcher running through the forests. Fletcher emerging out of the forests. Fletcher at the summit, on the raised dais. Fletcher, the universal panacea for all mankind.

The bands stopped. The ceremony was over. He must get a job, and he set off down the hill and bought a copy of the *Telegraph and Chronicle*.

7

TELEPHONISTS REQUIRED. APPLY IN WRITING TO Deputy Superintendant of Communications, Northern Lead Tubes Ltd., stating age, experience and details of National Automatic Dial Proficiency Tests passed.

Museum attendants wanted. Apply Box 80.

Are you an enthusiastic, ambitious and healthy university graduate, with an alert mind, a penchant for new gimmicks, a driving licence, and a solid grounding in the container production industry, who welcomes innovations, believes in expansion, can mix with industrial leaders, speaks Flemish, has advanced views on lid design and would be prepared to share bathroom with radiator mechanic? If so, apply Personnel Manager, the Conical Canister Corporation.

Applications are invited from those qualified to fill the post of CHIEF ENTOMOLOGIST at Badi El Swami Agricultural Research Centre, in the Republic of the Sudan. The selected officer would be expected to unify existing research on insect migration, and must have first-hand knowledge of tropical spiders and modern methods of aerial spray. Starting salary £1,750.

Spoon roughers and insiders, throstlers and large ingot men required. Apply British Watkinson Dessert Spoons and Sons.

Bus conductors required by City Corporation. Apply Ledge Street Garage.

Fletcher felt depressed after reading this list. It was not much use knowing that British Watkinson Dessert Spoons and Sons required spoon roughers and insiders, throstlers and large ingot men, unless you were a spoon rougher and insider, a throstler, or a large ingot man. But if you were any of these you would almost certainly have a job already, and so it was with every other one of the vacancies on the list. They demanded that you were already what they offered that you should become, and Fletcher, whose life consisted so largely of wanting to be what he was not, felt at a distinct disadvantage.

The only thing to do, he decided, was to apply for those jobs where the gap between their requirements and his capabilities seemed least. Obviously there was no chance of his becoming a Chief Entomologist, and he had never passed any Automatic Dial Proficiency Tests. He might have been designed as the direct opposite of what was required by the Conical Canister Corporation, and as for British Watkinson Dessert Spoons, he did not even know the meaning of most of the words in their advertisement.

No, it would have to be either a museum attendant or a bus conductor. It hardly mattered which, really. It was the fact of working, the fact of being of service, of fulfilling a function in the bustling city world, that mattered. Yet the fact that a decision is unimportant does not make it any easier to reach, and he was relieved when Mrs Pollard spoke.

"Not found much?" she asked.

"No. It seems to be either a bus conductor or a museum attendant."

"I don't know why you don't go back to teaching."

"I wasn't very successful as a teacher."

"I'm sorry to hear it."

"I couldn't cope."

"What a shame."

"So it seems to be either a bus conductor or a museum attendant."

"Very bad for the health, these museums. It's one thing to look round them and another thing to actually live there."

"Yes."

"I knew a man who worked in one. He caught Egyptology disease. He was very well preserved, for his years, but as dead as they come. It's his wife I'm sorry for. You never know how you might end up, if one of those places got a hold over you."

"Yes."

"Of course there are the treasures. You can't say that about a bus."

"No."

"You don't get the exhibits on a bus. Or the coins. It's just pennies, threepences and sixpences there. No variety. But then again you never know where you are with it in these museums. Roman coins, Saxon coins, everything."

"Yes."

"I mean you could go for the museums if you wanted to."

"Yes."

"But you know where you are on the buses. I'd choose the buses, if I were you."

8

THE INTERVIEW RAISED NO PROBLEMS AT ALL, MUCH to his surprise, and he formed the impression that it was easy to become a bus conductor, much easier than it was not to. The next morning he reported for training, and in common with about twenty-five other "new boys" he saw a series of films demonstrating the right and wrong ways of preventing dogs from sitting downstairs, ejecting spitters, recognising Irish coins and asking for the correct change without giving offence. Within two days he had been assigned to his route – the 92, from Woodlands to Pratts Lane Corner, via City – and had learned the fares between every fare stage on the route, in both directions.

On his first day of full duty he presented himself at the Ledge Street Garage at 5.27 a.m. It was a cold, windy morning, with flurries of tiny snowflakes. He was introduced to his driver, 3802 Driver Foster, a surly man who didn't even wave to the other drivers on his route, and then he entered the bus. He felt acutely conscious of himself in this strange uniform and wished only that the bus would open and swallow him up. When he was younger he had assumed that his nervousness would abate as he grew older. Now, when he was older, he found that his inexperience in each new job seemed even more noticeable and ludicrous, and he felt more nervous than ever.

Driver Foster started his engine with a cold ruthlessness that served only to mock his fears, and the great vehicle nosed slowly out of the garage and set off down the open road. At first there were only a few early-morning workers on the bus, but gradually it filled up with rush hour crowds and Fletcher's nervousness began to abate. He began to feel that joy which always came to him while working. He was in on the great struggle, helping. There was an orderly routine about his work which provided him with a sense of comfort and security. The duties were onerous enough to give him a constant sense of his usefulness without being so onerous as to induce nervous prostration. Up there in the grim loneliness of his cab Driver Foster treated each day as a battle, giving and asking no quarter and regarding it as a major defeat if he was forced to give way at a pedestrian crossing, especially to women with prams. In the crowded sociability of the lower and upper saloons, however, life was more than a battle. It was a crusade. Fletcher had suddenly realised that human life consists of a never-ending struggle to be in the right place at the right time. Each busload that he carried on the 92 route became, to his romantic imagination, a vital contribution towards ending that struggle. One day, if he worked hard, there would come a time of magic equilibrium, when everyone was already where he wanted to be.

And how hard he worked! What crowds he carried! He found it impossible to turn people away from his bus, when there was this great struggle to be won. He wanted to serve everyone, without distinction of class, creed, race or time of arrival. He believed in the freedom of the individual, pending the arrival of the purpose of existence.

Fletcher was thorough rather than swift. He found it difficult to collect all the fares even under normal conditions, and when his bus was particularly full he found it impossible. The rush hour crowds soon learnt that there was a distinct possibility of a free ride, and Fletcher's bus began to grow fuller still. Even more free rides were to be had, and even greater crowds were attracted. Soon the Inspector heard tales of the strange bus on route 92. He decided to inspect it.

The Inspector was a tall, tightly knit man, like an old walking stick, with grim caustic eyes set deep into his grizzle. Born to inspect, he had not been slow to do so. But he had never felt his sense of vocation so strongly as he did that cold windy morning, as he stood in front of the Pike House, waiting.

The Inspector signalled Fletcher's bus to a halt, and when he had boarded it – no easy matter, this, for the platform was crowded with passengers, he looked around for Fletcher. In vain. There was not a Fletcher to be seen. He noticed that none of the people who were thronging the corridor and stairs had any tickets, and the harsh gleam of inspection lit up his eyes. His face narrowed until it became as long as it had been broad, his eyes became slits and his lean nose was raised and thrust forward. He was a hound which had found the scent, and he would have bayed, had it been possible to do so with dignity.

"Where is the conductor?" he asked in a crisp, dry, thinly-sliced, unbuttered voice. A few heads turned slowly towards him and he repeated: "Where is the conductor?" There was something terrible about the man's inflexibility.

Nobody actually answered, but he formed the impression that

Fletcher was upstairs. It was obviously impossible for him to climb the stairs, packed as they were with travellers, so he clung desperately to the platform while he worked out how to deal with the problem. He was aware that for a majority of the passengers, including most of the younger ones and the old age pensioners, the crowding was a small price to pay for the pleasure of a free ride. He was aware, too, of a deep public resentment of his calling. People always took his presence on the bus as a personal affront to their integrity. He would have to tread warily, and, deeply though it pained him to let so much as a single twopenny juvenile fare be evaded, he realised that only when the bus was emptier would he be able to take any effective action. He judged that it would be impolitic to turn anyone off the bus, but that he could safely refuse to allow anyone else on without inflaming public prejudice.

By the time they reached the Goldplank Asylum and City Abattoir, living conditions had become tolerable again, and the Inspector was able to make his way upstairs. There he found Fletcher, looking stunned and exhausted by his work.

If Fletcher had looked stunned before, he was knocked flat when he saw the Inspector. He had an infinite capacity for being stunned.

"What is the meaning of this?" asked the Inspector. "Why was the bus so crowded? Why were so many fares uncollected?"

Fletcher, who was bending over to give an old lady her change, stood petrified in that position for a few moments. He felt as powerless, attempting to explain himself to this man, as a romantic lover might feel in trying to describe his emotions to a second row forward. But he knew that he must try, and slowly he rose to his full height, like an Indian rope trick. He looked the Inspector straight in the eyes and said: "I – er – that is."

"Yes?"

"I don't see why I should refuse people admission to this bus. They want to travel. I . . ."

"You what?"

"I have the means to enable them to travel."

"Oh, nice. Very nice. Very nice." The Inspector, suddenly leaning forward as if he was barely restraining himself from lifting Fletcher off the ground by his neck, barked: "Why don't you organise a running buffet into the bargain? Eh?"

"The passengers seemed happy enough," said Fletcher.

"What have they got to do with it?"

"I tried to give them what they needed."

The bus swung round into Riddings Close, and a cry of dismay rose from a thin-lipped man in a trilby.

"Why are we going down Riddings Close?" he wailed. "This is an 87, isn't it?"

"No," said the Inspector with relish, like an old spinster producing one last spade which nobody thought she'd got. "It's a 92."

"83," cried an old lady. "It says an 83."

"80."

"72."

"I thought it was a 75," volunteered a confectioner.

The Inspector immediately stopped the bus, his whole frame quivering with excitement. He used so little energy up in the rest of his life that he had a great surplus of intensity waiting in reserve for situations such as this. He got out of the bus and went round to the front.

The board indicated a 65, bound for Huggenthorpe! This was clearly false. The 65 went to Stoneytown Bridge, unless it was turned round at Sodge Moor Top. The Huggenthorpe bus was a 67, and in any case Huggenthorpe was in the opposite direction, beyond Market Edge. He stormed back to the bus in a carefully calculated fit of uncontrollable temper and confronted Fletcher, who was standing on the platform in great distress.

"Well?" said the Inspector, and waited patiently for a reply. Time was on his side.

"I don't understand it."

"Well I certainly don't." The Inspector led the way upstairs, and he immediately noticed that the four front seats were empty. Four youths, he remembered with the facility born of long experi-

31

ence, had been sitting there like a display of barrack room brooms. The back of the indicator board – one of the old type that are adjusted from upstairs – was open. He turned towards Fletcher.

"You left the indicator board unlocked. That's what's happened. Those four youths have changed the board between each stop. You see what happens when you let too many people on a bus."

The public, their free journeys forgotten, turned on the man whom they held responsible. Ugly mutterings arose, and the Inspector, his triumph complete, felt able to protect his conductor from their threats.

When he had quietened the passengers the Inspector made a brief inquiry and found that only ten of the passengers were bound for stops on the 92 route. Routes on which passengers believed themselves to be travelling included the 87, 83, 80, 77, 75, 72, 68 and 65.

His inquiry over, the Inspector apologised to the passengers and told them that their tickets would be valid for the return journey to the City, where they could catch their proper buses. He informed the passengers who wanted the 92 route that they would have to wait for the next bus, as Fletcher had developed a defect and was being taken out of service. They grunted, as if to imply that it was not his fault, and then, casting ugly glances at Fletcher, they stepped out into the snow.

The Inspector went round to the cab and spoke to Driver Foster. "Why did you do nothing about all this, Foster?" he asked.

"All what, sir?" asked Driver Foster.

"All this overcrowding on the bus," said the Inspector.

"I obey the bells, sir. Two rings, and I start. One ring, and I stop. Three rings, bus running to full capacity. And I've never once had three rings. Two, one, but not three. I've never once had the bell that indicated to me: 'Bus running to full capacity.' So there's never been any reason for me to bother with overcrowding."

"Drive us back to the garage, Foster," said the Inspector.

Fletcher and the Inspector sat side by side in the empty bus as they drove to the garage. Only a few sweet papers and cigarette ends bore witness to the fact that the bus had ever served a useful purpose in society – or ever would again.

"I'm taking you to see the Chief Inspector, Fletcher," said the Inspector.

"Yes, sir."

"Why can't you be more like Foster?" the Inspector asked sadly.

Fletcher could think of no reply.

9

"THIS IS AN ODD BUSINESS, FLETCHER," SAID CHIEF Inspector Wilkins, and even as he spoke Fletcher felt that this was a man to whom he would be able to talk.

"I wanted to serve," he said.

"There's nothing wrong in that, though it has never appealed to me," said the Inspector. "But who did you want to serve?"

"Everyone."

"That explains why there were 215 people on your bus, does it?"

"Well, sir, I don't see why I should refuse anyone admission."

"The bus might become overcrowded. Didn't that occur to you?" Fletcher was silent, and the Chief Inspector continued: "Injuries might have occurred. Fire might have broken out in those crowded conditions. Didn't you think of that?" Ninety-nine Chief Inspectors out of a hundred would have confined themselves to the regulations and attempted to have Fletcher certified. Chief Inspector Wilkins – although he had never let anyone suspect it, especially his wife, to whom he was happily married – was the hundredth man in any gathering.

"I don't see who I could refuse to admit?"

"You are supposed to allow five standing."

"But which five? If one five, why not another?" There was a brief pause. The Chief Inspector, man in a hundred though he was, felt justified in being taken aback. "Why not ten, fifteen, twenty, twenty-five, sir?"

"Or four hundred and twenty-five, Fletcher. You have to stop somewhere. There isn't room for everybody. We stop at five."

"But you still have to decide which five, sir."

"You should allow the first five on. It's only fair."

"I'm afraid I can't agree with you, sir," said Fletcher. He was frightened of saying this, but there could be no stopping, now that he had taken the plunge.

"No?"

"It seems very unfair to penalise the second five for the fact that there are already five people on the bus. The first five are entirely to blame for that."

There was a pause, which the Chief Inspector broke very lamely. "It is necessary to have rules sometimes, you know," he said.

Fletcher said nothing. He was not convinced, nor was Chief Inspector Wilkins.

"I'm going to tell you something," said the Chief Inspector. "I have never myself regarded buses as being for the use of the public. I don't think it's hard-heartedness, although as I told you the idea of service has never appealed to me. I think I like the public tolerably well, on the whole. I wish them well, generally speaking. But I have never been able to accept, in my heart of hearts, that buses are functional. I love them. I love them for themselves. You understand what I mean?"

"Yes, sir."

"I love my wife, I suppose, but I love buses more. Hilda's a very good woman, in her way, and we get on well, but you couldn't love her for herself. I love her for her meals, her children, the home she runs. Take all that away and our marriage would collapse. But buses are different. I'd like to drive them around empty. I like their elegant, gently sloping fronts and their comforting square radiators. I – well, I love them. It's monstrous that they should be used to carry people to cemeteries and supermarkets. Monstrous. Quite, quite monstrous." Chief Inspector Wilkins recovered himself and resumed in a more conversational, less emotional manner. "I once wrote a paper arguing that the public were a penance paid by all bus people for the original sin implicit in the erection of the first bus stop. That sort of thing doesn't go down too well in Omnibus Mansions. My attitude to buses is oriental. I admire their purity, their serenity, their detachment. Press the self starter and all that is lost." He smiled at Fletcher. "I've kept all this to myself for twenty years, and now I've told you, so you see you have achieved something," he said. Fletcher smiled back, shyly, and the Chief Inspector continued. "Yes, Fletcher, I was forced to admit, for the purpose of my life on earth, that buses have a function. If I'd told anyone what I've told you, I'd have been certified. One has to be careful, Fletcher, and that goes for you too, you know. So, please, go away, get another job, and be careful." The Chief Inspector stood up and held out his hand. "I've spoken to you as a man. Now I appeal to you as a Chief Inspector. You're fired. You'll get a week's pay in lieu of notice."

Fletcher felt immeasurably betrayed. He had told this man of his opinions openly and without hesitation, and that was a miracle. He had listened to a confidence without embarrassment, and that was a miracle too. And then he had been sacked. As he went out into the late morning he felt a broken man. The sky was the colour of slush, and the wind was cold, and there was one week's pay in his pocket, as he tacked through the cold, grey nothing.

IO

"WHAT I ALWAYS SAY," SAID MRS POLLARD, "IS THAT if a man can't face these setbacks with a smile he isn't a man."

Fletcher faced this setback with a thin, wan smile. Mrs Pollard, who had seen little of him during the past fortnight, what with his shift work and everything, had been surprised to see him back so early, but she had not been nearly so surprised when he told her that he had lost his job. She had given the impression that she had known all along that he wasn't the man for bus conducting. There was something, she let it be felt, too intelligent about him. It was not that he had told her anything about his schemes, but she had not failed to notice his studious and distant manner in the evenings. There had been nothing she could do. It had been man's work, and Mrs Pollard had been a landlady far too long to interfere with that. She knew that she must wait until the moment came for her to swing into action, and that when the moment did finally come she must swing with all her might.

"I'll have a nice bowl of stew ready for you in a jiffy," she said. "Pollard always used to say there's nothing like a nice hot stew to cheer a man when he's down. Warm the stomach and you warm the heart."

While Mrs Pollard was making the stew, Fletcher sat before his table, as motionless as possible, patiently awaiting the upsurge of some new emotion. Very soon he found himself in a silent world. He rolled the silence smoothly round his brain. It was a silence that might never end. It was his own silence, his great eternity, in which he might sit whenever he wanted, in his usual chair. Whenever the mood took him, whenever he felt unusually battered and bruised, he could return to it and find himself sitting there. As a point of reference it had few equals, but as a refuge it had a draw-

36

back. It could be – and invariably was – interrupted. Perhaps he would never know what had interrupted it, and he would slide gently out of the silence. He would hear all the noises of the world as if they were far away, but coming closer, and he would begin to feel, faintly at first, like the light from the distant opening of a tunnel, his hunger. And then it would get nearer and nearer until he was suddenly out again in the sunlight, fully exposed to all his needs and fears.

On this occasion he did know what had interrupted it. It was Mrs Pollard, coming in to tell him: "It's about the stew. It's not coming along too well."

"What?"

"It's about the stew. It's not coming along too well."

"Oh, dear."

"There are things in it that I wouldn't advise. You know how it is. I thought it was going to be one kind of stew and then I realised that it was going to be a completely different sort. And now it's got stuck at the awkward stage, and I don't quite know what to do." She paused, and then, when nothing happened, she went on: "I wondered if you'd come and have a look. It takes a man to understand these things."

A ruse, to secure him to her boudoir! Well, why not go? It would be nice to sit by her fire. These coal ranges were quite delightful, and there was no time to lose. Soon they would be making it into a smokeless zone. Go then. Blossom forth. Old smokeless Fletcher, thirty-nine, of no fixed coal fire, be off with you.

But after all he had only known her for a matter of a few weeks. And it might be that she really did want his advice on the stew. A fine fool he'd look, in that case. What advice could he possibly give?

On the other hand if it was just to give some advice, well, there was no harm in that. Wise old Fletcher, what advice you could give if you put your mind to it!

No. She would make demands on him. He would be drawn in, closer and closer. He would become a part of her hearth, and of her life. He had not had time to think much of Mrs Pollard since his work had begun, but now there was time and as he thought about her his uneasiness returned. He wanted to be away from her, safe and free, out of the house, out of her reach, out on the open road, far from the open fire.

And yet to accept an invitation to advise her on a stew could hardly be said to commit him to anything. There would be no question of intimacy. A curt piece of advice, an ingredient or two suggested, and ta-ta for now. It would be churlish to refuse, and besides, it would suggest that he had read into the invitation more than was there.

So he decided that he would go. He thought he would rise from his chair, but he didn't. He thought that perhaps if he applied an absence of pressure to his buttocks and raised the top of his head towards the ceiling, he might stand up. But it was not to be, and for about forty minutes he remained seated. Mrs Pollard left long before the end.

And then, just when he had given up all hope, he was on his feet. He was at the door, opening it. He was in the corridor, and once there he had either to walk down it or to return to his room, which seemed foolish. So he walked down it, and knocked on the kitchen door.

"Come in," said Mrs Pollard. She was standing over the casserole, and she smiled when she saw him. "I thought you were never coming," she said.

Stiff with self-consciousness, Fletcher walked over to the bubbling, aromatic cauldron and gazed into its depths. "It looks very good," he said.

"But it isn't finished."

"I'm hungry."

"It needs improving."

"No. It's all right."

"It would have been such a lovely stew," said Mrs Pollard, with an air of grumpy wistfulness more suited to a schoolgirl.

"I know." For a moment their eyes met, but Fletcher quickly lowered his and the moment was gone. His heart was beating fast and he was on the verge of panicking.

38

"I'll get my table ready," he said, and he walked towards the door.

"Won't you have it in here, then?"

"No, I – really." He left the room as slowly as he dared, and rushed to his room. His hands were shaking.

Mrs Pollard followed with the stew, and to his annoyance she once again remained in his room.

"You aren't happy, are you?" she asked with startling suddenness.

"Well, I've just lost my job."

"There are plenty more."

"I had hopes. Little hopes, you know. It's always a shock when they come to nothing."

"If there's anything I can do . . ."

"No. That's all right. It's very kind of you. I just need a bit of quiet, that's all."

"What you need is another job. It's no use moping."

"Not yet. A bit of quiet makes a new man of me. I'll just stay here for a while, being quiet, if you don't mind. Nothing serious, you know. Just a week or two."

"Well, you know best, I suppose. Though there are some that don't. Some of you bachelors. If you ask me you ought to be out and about a bit, even if it's only the pictures. It's not right for a grown man like you to just sit there."

"I shan't be just sitting. I'd rather call it a period of recreation."

"You call it what you like, and I'll listen. Well, I'll leave you in peace, then, if you've finished your meal."

Don't go. Don't leave me alone. Don't fluster me. Go.

"Yes," said Fletcher.

"I'll be off and see to Mr Veal." She walked slowly to the door with the casserole. "Anyway," she said awkwardly, "you'll know where to find me, if you want me. And don't say I didn't warn you."

Left to himself, Fletcher found that he was thinking of Veal. He wondered why he never saw the man, and he felt jealous. Why were they never allowed to meet? What did Mrs Pollard do on her visits to him?

It was only when he caught sight of himself in the hexagonal glass mirror which hung above the mantelshelf that he managed to forget these questions. The mirror had cut-glass borders, and in the borders he could see a thousand faces, long, short and twisted, faces with five mouths and four chins, square mouths and round mouths and oval mouths and some with no mouths at all, all staring back at him with looks of grotesque horror.

He stood up, and placed himself in front of the mirror, with his eyes shut. All he had to do was to open those eyes of his and gaze straight into the centre of the mirror. He began to lower the pressure on his lids, and the black became tinged with red. Open them! He felt his brain giving out the order. He could feel an opening of his eyes travelling slowly from his brain towards his eyes, but before it could reach them a hasty command was issued to them to remain shut. A series of commands followed, and each time he could feel the command to remain shut catching up with the command to open. He was blind.

And then his eyes were open, as if they had never been shut. They were gazing at the centre of the mirror, and the face that met them was his own. The cheeks were pale and rather hollow, he had not shaved well, his hair was receding, there were a few blackheads on his nose, and in the centre of his chin there was one white-headed pimple.

There were signs of approaching age in the lines on his face. Soon he would be too old to be mothered, as in the past he had been mothered by all those mothers of his. All of them, all except one, they had all been mothering him. Just one there had been who had not been mothering him, who had threatened him with something more than that. It had been fifteen years ago, when he was Lewis. He'd been fifteen years younger then.

He sat down again. Separated from him only by two doors sat Mrs Pollard with her memories, and with her expectations. The logs glowed. Now she rose and bent over the fire, her outline illuminated for nobody to see by the sudden jumping of the flames she had disturbed as she heaped the wood. Then she sat again, with her knitting and her thoughts. What did she think of? What could she possibly knit? She threatened him, there could be no escaping the fact. She wanted him to be more than a son. How desirable all those past years seemed to Fletcher, with all those mothers. He began again to think about his mothers, and of that night, long ago, when he was Lewis.

I I

MOTHER HAD BEEN THE FIRST. SHE HAD BEEN KIND and gentle, or at least he assumed, from the photographs, that she had been kind and gentle. She had died young, and then there had been Aunt Emily, who lived all alone in Worcestershire, with a hoe, a rake, and natural foods. What Aunt Emily had lacked in affection she had made up for in Cash's name tapes. She had equipped him with all that she took to be the necessities of life – clothes and initials – and had packed him off to his next mother, Winchester.

At the old Alma Mater his trousers had grown longer and longer, his memory shorter and shorter, and they had cried: "Manners will make a man of him yet."

Then came the war and his spell in the Pay Corps, where s.q.m.s. Wadhurst had been the nearest approach to a mother, without getting significantly close. Next he had been packed off to Cambridge, his education paid for by a father he had never seen. With parents as with everything else he had failed to strike a proper balance. Mothers all along the line, and never a father in sight.

During his first year at Cambridge he had lived in college, and nobody had taken the slightest notice of him, but after that he moved into lodgings and found another mother – Mrs Violet, just off the Trumpington Road. Mrs Violet had had such a nice boy the year before, a Mr Tompkin-Leverett, who had been a bit of a one but always a gentleman. Mrs Violet had said, without conviction; "I'll make a Tompkin-Leverett of you yet."

And so he had gone out into the world, with all its challenges and its opportunities and its unlimited supply of mothers. There had been Miss Potter, washing his socks and advising him on matters of spiritualism. There had been Mrs McManus, of Barnstaple, keeping up his strength with regular milk drinks and keeping him *au fait* with affairs "on the other side". There had been Mrs McManus of Newport (I.O.W.), helping him to buy really durable underclothes, Swiss style, and telling him all about her experiences in other realms. And there had been so many others that he could hardly distinguish them from each other. He had had a large number of employers in his time, but they paled to insignificance beside his mothers.

His thoughts turned to the one young woman who had not been a mother, when he was Lewis. Miss Daisy Wilkinson had been her name, and it was partly her youth that had prevented her from being a mother. She had floated into his life by accident one night, and almost immediately she had floated out of it again, but he remembered that night as vividly as if it had been the week before.

There had been snow for several hours. He was sitting motionless in the corner seat next to the window, facing the engine, and she was sitting motionless in the corner seat next to the window, facing him. The train had been delayed for several minutes and it was this that brought them into conversation.

"Where are we?" she asked.

"I – I don't know."

"Nor me." Her mouth was small and her hair was black and her small breasts fixed beady eyes on him out of a green sweater. She had unusually well defined knees, and despite the cold she had allowed the neck of the sweater to fall a little, so that Lewis could admire the white boniness of her shoulders, should he so desire.

"Somewhere, I suppose," he said.

"Like something to read?" she asked.

"No, thanks. I can't read in trains."

They stared at the fog together, and Lewis felt trapped, leaving so much unsaid. He felt that he was having thoughts, even though he was too confused to realise them. He even felt uneasy at having thought them without feeling clear-headed enough to realise that some of his uneasiness was inspired by guilt.

"I'll be late," she said.

"You're going home?" he asked. The breathlessness in his voice must be painfully apparent to her, yet she made no reference to it, thus convincing him that it must be as terrible to her as a disfigurement.

"Yes. I live at home. Bromley. It's not too bad. Mummy and Daddy are very nice."

"That's nice."

"What is?"

"Your mummy and daddy."

"You don't know them."

"I expect it's the snow."

"You are funny."

"Me?"

"There's no-one else in the carriage."

As if he was not aware of that!

"You expect what's the snow?"

"All this waiting."

"Of course it is, fool."

At this moment the train took pity on Lewis and clanked into motion. His brain was working like an automaton below his confusion and he stared rigidly out of the window at nothing. Soon the outskirts of a city could be made out through the dark night, and he recorded the brightly-lit names of the factories out loud.

"Midland Accessory Company," he murmured. She did not respond to that one, and they rode on in silence for a while.

"Leadbetter and Platt – the best in wicker baskets," he said.

"What?"

"What? Oh, it's just a factory."

There was a pause.

"You've not got much small talk," she said. "You must be thinking of something very important."

"No, I . . . in a way."

"I'd like to hear about it," she said.

The train had stopped again and he wondered whether he should risk stepping out into the snow.

"You don't mind my asking, do you?"

"No. No." They were on the middle line of four, in so far as that was possible. If another train came . . . and then the train began to move again, with a tremendous jerk and a prolonged rattling and crashing that roared past the carriage in waves before being muffled in scarves of snow. To jump now would be fatal, and there was so much left for him to do. He could hardly duck out of his responsibilities now.

"We're moving," he said.

"I think perhaps I'll get out at the next station and ring them up from there, and tell them I can't get home tonight," she said. "There must be a station with all these factories."

"Twelve," he said.

"Twelve what?"

"Miles an hour."

"How do you know?"

"You work it out from the noise of the wheels and the telegraph poles and things."

"Honestly?"

"Yes."

"You are clever."

"Swinnertons Surplus Boots."

"Where are you getting out?"

"I – I don't know."

"You must know where you're going."

"I'm not going anywhere in particular. I'm just on the move."

"You're touring, in this weather?"

44

"No. I've stayed in one place and it didn't work out and now I'm going somewhere else."

"What do you do?"

"Oh, all sorts of things."

"Don't tell me then."

"I used to be a seismographer's assistant."

"A what?"

"A deputy recorder of earthquakes."

"Golly. Why did you give it up?"

"I was sacked."

"I'm sorry. What will you do now?"

Why not tell her? Why not describe to her all about the purpose of existence?

"The Bronze Gong Company."

"You'll work there?"

"What? No, I don't know. I don't know what I'll do."

"What's your name?"

"Hewitt – *the* name for stomach pumps."

"What?"

"We've just passed it."

"I asked you what your name was."

"Lewis."

"And your first name?"

"I only have the one."

"That's stingy. Mine's Daisy. Daisy Wilkinson. How do you do, Lewis."

"How do you do, Daisy?" She shook his hand and smiled at him, but she did not take her hand away again and when he tried to withdraw his she clung to it and smiled again.

"Leicester Midland Number One Signal Box."

"Leicester. Get out here with me."

The train ran gently into the deserted station and stopped with a slight jerk.

"Come on, Lewis," she said.

"I'm not getting out here."

"We may as well. The train may get snowed up."

"It's stopped."

"It may start again. Oh, come on, Lewis." She stood up and began to gather together her belongings, such as they were. "There's no point in being stuck all night in a train."

"You go, then."

"I'm frightened."

"I'm not coming," he said dumbly. He was in a muck sweat and he felt like an obstinate schoolboy. If he had been the next to speak he would have said: "So there," but luckily he wasn't.

Daisy clutched frantically at him, and her lips met what would have been his cheek, had it not by that time been the back of his neck.

"Come on," she said. "Please. I'm all alone."

"No."

His darling Daisy was pulling him to his feet, and it was exciting to resist her playfully, to feel her little tendons straining away at him, knowing that it was all a game and soon she would have him out on the platform in the cold, all to herself, and later, in a sumptuous room, scented with delicious perfumes, the deep silence of the cold night disturbed only by the rhythmic clanking of the A.A. and R.A.C. signs outside their window, and later still, in their cottage, together, with the windows open and the scent of the honeysuckle, the hammering of woodpeckers in a distant grove, the . . .

"Oh, come on."

Later.

He seemed to move and remain stationary at the same time. There were tears in her eyes, and her hands fell limp, and as he slid through them, back into his seat, striking his head upon the sharpest part of an ashtray, he realised that he had no idea yet whether or not he would leave the train with her. All he had to do was stand up, but he didn't. Nothing had been decided.

There was still time. But the waves of indecision brought with them the nausea of terror, and then he knew that he would not leave the train. Not at Leicester, anyway. Some day, somewhere, he might leave the train, but not now. It was a great relief, and

46

he knew that he had made the right decision. With his defects he could never protect her.

Lewis was in fact exaggerating these defects. There were respects, it is true, in which he plumbed new depths – conversation, armpits and muscles, for instance – but these were offset by those points in which he excelled – thickness of neck, size in shoes and teeth, etc.

"I must move on further," he said.

"Why?"

"I told you. I've got to make a fresh start."

"You can do that here."

"It doesn't feel far enough away."

"You can move on tomorrow."

"No. It's no use putting things off." His answers were by no means inspired, but at least his brain, impelled by the seriousness of the situation, was providing something instead of just folding up, as was so often the case when it was most needed.

She made no further comment, and he fixed his attention on a speck of dust on the floor. It moved barely perceptibly at the faint impact of their breath. There was no other air in the compartment.

"I'll stay with you," said Daisy, and at first the words were mere sounds. Then, when the train set off, they took on meaning. Lewis felt a touch of claustrophobia coming on. "I couldn't get off all alone in a strange town at this time of night."

"I don't mind," he said, his kindness overcoming his horror for a moment, and she smiled at him sweetly.

After they had travelled on in silence for a short while, Daisy said: "I work in an office", as if to rebuke him for not asking her what she did.

"What do you do?"

"Oh, just forms."

"Do you like it?"

"No."

Lewis was sorry. Suddenly he wanted to talk to her about something interesting, to bring colour into her life. He'd heard lectures, read newspapers, listened to broadcasts, seen plays, attended symposia. He'd travelled, and he wanted to tell her of all the places that he'd seen – Solihull, Ventnor, everywhere. But no. His past seemed like an orgy of volubility now, however cramped it had felt at the time. Now, as she sat waiting for him to begin, he could think of nothing to say. What a mind they had fobbed him off with.

"I've some sandwiches," he said at last. "Would you like one? They're ham," and she smiled at him, believing the battle to be half won.

"Yes, please."

He stood up and took his suitcase from the rack. There, securely wrapped in his pyjamas, were the sandwiches. He took them out, repacked the pyjamas and put the suitcase back on the rack. Then with shaking fingers he removed the paper from the sandwiches and handed her one. They ate. It was as if they had made a tacit agreement not to mention the pyjamas.

After they had eaten, they journeyed on in a silence that was broken only occasionally by little flurries of conversation. These were mainly fatuous, and it was a great surprise to Lewis, who was too wrapped up in his own confusion to be aware what Daisy was feeling, when she suddenly began to cry.

"What's wrong?" he said. No man could have said less.

"You don't like me."

"What?" He was appalled, and was torn between sympathy and horror at the necessity of doing something about it.

"There's nothing wrong with me, is there?"

"Of course not."

"I'm not particularly intelligent but I mean I'm not the dumb kind, am I? I'm not the sort of person to forget the horrors and inhumanities of war in the excitement and anguish of growing into a woman. I mean give me fun every time, but I'm not just a good time girl. What I mean is, I'm a member of the Young Conservatives but I don't see why I should be T.T. or anything. And I like art, even if I don't know much about it, and I can sew and mend socks and read shorthand. I'm quite useful really."

"There's nothing wrong with you. Now try and get some sleep."

"What?"

"I'm tired."

She began to cry again, and he took hold of her hand and patted it. That much was forced upon him by the exigencies of the situation. She came and sat beside him, and she said: "I'm being silly."

"You're tired. It's very late."

"Yes." She stopped crying. The train had stopped again, and they found themselves looking out of the window at the deep banks of snow, their faces close together. "You're shaking," she said. Her hands were round his waist, feeling it gently, and her head was in his lap. It was very strange behaviour, he thought, on the part of such a young Conservative, and quite intolerable now that she had finished crying. "Are you cold?" she asked.

"No."

"You're rather bony, aren't you?"

He began to giggle.

"You're laughing," she said in an injured tone.

"I'm not. I'm ticklish." She stopped moving her hands, but continued to hold him tightly. He would burst. That was what he would do. That would put the cat among the pigeons. "You'll have to let go," he managed to say, and to his surprise she did so. "Get some sleep," he said gently, and for a few minutes they travelled through the early night of life together, boy and girl, unable to sleep.

Girl, as so often, was the first to speak.

"A penny for them," she said, with an attempt at cheerfulness.

"I was thinking," said Lewis, shivering.

"What about?" asked Daisy.

"Life."

"Oh." There was a pause, and he shivered again. "It's gone very cold," she said, and she got up and began to fiddle with the heating handle. "We seem to have run out of heat. I don't understand these things, do you?"

"No."

For a minute or two they wrestled with the heater, and eventually they left it in the "off" position. Lewis felt that other couples would laugh gaily about not understanding the heating handle, and he wished that they could laugh gaily as well.

Soon steam began to rise from under the seats and the air became heavy with warmth. The lids of their eyes grew heavy, and it was not long before they were asleep.

"Nodding off, eh?" said Mrs Pollard, bursting in upon his past without knocking. "I'm not surprised, with such a fug in here. It's not healthy, say what you will."

Fletcher said what he would, which was, "No."

"They never know how to look after themselves, authors."

"I'm not an author," said Fletcher, yawning.

"No. Well, you certainly don't know how to look after yourself. I came to say that I'm for bed and are you wanting the bottle now? It's on."

"What time is it?"

"Ten to twelve."

"Yes, thank you. I shan't be long."

Mrs Pollard fetched him his bottle, and placed it on the floor. He thanked her for it and she said good night and he said: "Good night. I'm sorry I'm so tired."

"And why shouldn't you be?" said Mrs Pollard in surprise.

"No, I, I thought for the moment that you were someone else." Mrs Pollard stared at him. "I was elsewhere."

"I'll give you elsewhere."

Left to himself, Fletcher grabbed hold of the sofa and wrenched it into a bed in a series of convulsive, screeching jerks. Then he cleaned his teeth, undressed, placed his clothes untidily over the back of the wooden chair, tightened the cord of his pyjamas, put the bottle into the bed, and crept in after it. Then he crept out of bed, switched off the fire, and crept back in again.

He lay there silently, staring miserably at the ceiling. Occasionally the sinuous body of his landlady flashed across his mind. Occasionally the train stopped at another station, and Daisy stirred. And then, sooner than he expected, the stations and Daisy and his landlady died away, and he began to grow smaller. Smaller and smaller he grew, until he could see himself, a tiny figure deep down at the back of his eyes. He was rushing towards himself, growing smaller and smaller all the time, and by the time he arrived at his vast great bed he was minute. Soon he would cross the borders of consciousness. He grew smaller and smaller and smaller, and in the end he disappeared.

12

HE WAS SEATED IN FRONT OF THE MIRROR WHEN THE summons came. He had slept deeply, and was feeling very refreshed, as he sat in front of the mirror, realising his personality.

First there was the knock on the door. Two hortative raps.

"Come in," he said.

Then the door opened and the person who had knocked began to appear. When assembled inside the room he was seen to be a tall, well-proportioned, clean-shaven young man, handsome in a rather masculine way, with a strong chin, frank blue eyes, fair wavy hair, firm well-modulated lips and a high, intelligent forehead. In short, a police constable.

"Good morning, Mr Simpson," said the constable.

"I – er – good morning, officer. Please sit down if you can find . . . if only I'd known you were . . . I live alone and you know how things . . . won't you take off your . . . but I suppose you aren't allowed to on duty. Simpson?"

"Yes, sir."

"SIMPSON?"

"Yes, sir."

"I see. Well, what can I do for you?"

"I'm sorry to have to trouble you at a time like this, Mr Simpson, but I'm a search party." He blushed. He was not long out of police school. He lived on one of the new estates with his mother, who looked after him well, washing his hairbrush each week so that he wouldn't go bald before his time and making sure that he spread his socks with anti-fungoid powder each morning, so that his feet wouldn't rot and make him too short for the force. Everyone brushed their hair and washed their feet on the estate. They were nice people.

"Oh."

"Yes, and I have a search warrant for your arrest." He blushed furiously.

"I – search?"

"It's just a formality, sir, before we arrest you."

"I see. Well, we'll have to do it in here, I'm afraid. Mrs Pollard, you see. I find her very reasonable."

"But you don't want to presume?"

"No. I think I'll lock the door. Yes, the food is not at all bad, though I suppose digs are never quite the same thing, are they, officer?"

"I suppose not, sir."

"I've spent all my life in digs."

"Not married, sir?"

"No." It was Simpson's turn to blush now. "I did think of it once. It's a long time ago now. Shall we start, and get it over?"

"Yes, sir. I'll search your pockets first."

"Right. Yes, it seemed a long time ago, even then."

"I don't see many girls, not in my life."

"No. This arrest, officer. Do you know what it's for?"

"Not until I read the charge out, sir, and I can't do that until the search is complete."

"I see."

"You're taking it very calmly, sir."

"I don't understand it yet."

"I – I'm afraid I shall have to undress you now." Once more the blushes ran down the constable's face and under his tunic, where they couldn't be seen. "I'm very sorry about this, sir."

"So am I." Simpson managed a faint smile. "You have your job to do." There was a pause. "I'll feel better when I know what I've done."

"Won't be long now, sir."

"Ouch."

"I'm sorry, sir. I've forgotten to cut my nails."

"Easily done, I should imagine, officer."

"I'm afraid so, sir."

"Very easily."

"Not bad weather, sir?"

"Not bad."

"An awful lot of snow, though."

"Yes."

"Still, it's always the same in these parts."

"I'm a stranger here."

"Are you, sir? So am I. We come from London."

"Oh. London."

"Which parts do you come from, sir?"

"I – ouch."

"Sorry."

"Leeds and Margate and Barnstaple and the Isle of Wight."

"Oh. Those parts."

"Yes."

"You have to move around in your job, sir?"

"It isn't so much that." He was fully undressed now. The constable, very embarrassed, looked him up and down and then began to shake all his clothes. "Some day I may settle down, when I've found what I'm looking for."

"You're looking for something, sir?"

"Yes."

"What is it, sir? Buried treasure? X marks the spot?"

"Ouch."

"Sorry."

"No, it's nothing like that." There was a pause.

"Anyway I hope you find it, sir," said the constable.

"Thank you. I hope so too."

53

"You can put your clothes on now, sir."

"Oh, thank you, officer."

"I really am very sorry, sir. I hope you weren't too cold."

"Not at all. It just couldn't be helped. Did you find anything?"

"No, sir."

"Nothing at all?"

"No, sir."

"I suppose it all depends what you're looking for."

That must be it, thought the constable. Goodness knows what he was looking for though. They hadn't told him that. Perhaps it was just as well, under the circumstances, that he'd found nothing.

"Do you like your work?" Simpson asked, as he put on his socks.

"No, sir. I regard it as an occupational hazard."

"How long have you been doing it?"

"Nearly six months now, sir. It's not too bad I suppose. There are moments when I quite enjoy it. Then at other times I begin to wonder. I mean, some of the things you have to do are pretty awful. Arrests, for instance. And whipping people to make them confess. You begin to wonder whether you're cut out for the job. It's not as if I had a calling for it."

"Well, officer, I wish you the best of luck anyway." Simpson, fully dressed again, proffered his hand. The constable shook it. Then he began to blush again.

"Are you ready, sir?" he asked.

"Ready? Oh, of course. Just let me brush my hair." Simpson brushed his hair and removed a few loose hairs from his jacket. "Right."

"You are charged," read the constable, "that on the night of January 9 to 10 last in Corporation Street of this city you did wilfully, maliciously and without authority utter obscene documents and melodies, and also that at the same time and place you did wilfully and with malice aforethought park your wife, Esme Simpson, upon a bombed site, contrary to the Spouse Protection Act of 1623. You are further charged that on January 10 you did wilfully and maliciously kidnap with intent one Gertrude Walsh, of Thresher's Farm, and did behave in a manner liable to cause a breach of promise." Simpson went very white and sank into a chair. The constable put an arm on his shoulder. "I must warn you that everything you say will be taken down and may be used in evidence against you," he said.

"Is that all?"

"Yes, sir."

Simpson sighed deeply, while the constable handcuffed him as gently as possible. They went to the bathroom together and the constable poured a glass of water, which Simpson drank. Then Simpson poured a glass of water, which the officer drank.

They set off towards the police station then. All his life Simpson had summoned up ecstasy by clasping his hands together and exerting violent pressure upon them. Now all he wanted to do was to fling them apart. The pain of not being able to do so was almost insufferable in his arms and in his head.

Suddenly the constable stopped.

"That charge, sir," he said. "I thought you said you weren't married."

Simpson shrugged his shoulders. The constable shrugged his. But for the handcuffs they would have shrugged each other's.

"I thought I'd better mention it, sir," said the constable.

"That's all right, officer."

"I'm sorry about all this, sir."

"So am I."

Their feet beat a muffled path upon the snow.

"I'm sure it'll turn out all right, sir," said the constable.

13

SIMPSON COULD FEEL NO GUILT. IT WAS AS IF THE
crimes had been committed by some other man. He felt that if
he could recall them he would be able to defend himself adequately, but he could not recall them. In the absence of any alternative defence he secured legal aid, and although his application
for bail was refused – it appeared that he had a bad record – he
had plenty of opportunity to confer with his lawyer, Mr C. T.
Ackroyd.

Mr Ackroyd was the son of old E. K. Ackroyd, the golfer, of
Braithwaite, Ackroyd, and Clegg. He was a tall, cold-shouldered
man, with an air of having cut his body to suit his cloth, and
Simpson disliked him from the start. There was something un-
natural about his manner.

"Well now, my man, what's all this?" he had begun. "Quite
a night, eh? Been on the beer, had you? What were you celebra-
ting? Managed to get a divorce or something? Ha ha ha, eh?"

"I don't remember a thing," said Simpson coldly.

"I shouldn't think you would, in the state you must have been
in. Ha ha ha ha ha, eh? Still, we aren't here to discuss that." He
sat down on the hard chair which had been provided for him, and
withdrew from his briefcase a wad of papers. "Now then, let's get
down to brass tacks, shall we?" he said in a manner slightly less
hearty. "You'll have to listen to what I say pretty carefully, and
I want you to take care how you answer. All right? Good. We're
going to have to go pretty deep. It's going to be a pretty deep
case. Parkinson-Hoddinott will see to that. Likes to burrow, does
Parkinson-Hoddinott. Great fellow. Played fives with his brother.
But he's deep. You have to be careful with him. Charming fellow
socially, but he can be an absolute stinker in the courts. Ha ha
ha, eh? It's the Hoddinott in him coming out. They're an old

56

legal family. Old Augustus Hoddinott, the cricketer, slow left arm, prosecuted in the Barnsley Leather Satchel Case, when I was a student. But I didn't come here to talk about that, did I? My point is, to handle old P.H. we've got to have our psychological stuff pretty well mapped out. He's very fair on that side, old P.H. I don't mind telling you, Simpson old man, that if we could prove that this whole show was pathological it would be a load off my mind."

Although Ackroyd did not mind telling him, Simpson appeared to mind being told. Throughout this address he had sat motionless, looking as pathological as he had ever done in his life. His expression did not suggest that it was a great load off his mind.

"I think the thing to do is to delve around in your old subconscious," went on Ackroyd. "After all, it sounds as though you were pretty well subconscious most of the time you were doing these things. Ha ha ha ha, eh?" Ackroyd paused, with the self-satisfied air of a man who has done his bit pretty adequately and can now wait for some comment to be passed. But Simpson, who had been given no chance of answering a series of questions which he had been forced to regard as rhetorical, did not reply. He would wait for a question demanding an answer, and until then he would hold his peace.

"You won't mind if I ask you a few questions, will you, old man?" asked Ackroyd.

Simpson waited a moment, found that the question demanded an answer, and replied.

"No," he said.

"They may seem pretty simple to you, but they're important, so please answer carefully. O.K.?"

"Yes."

"Good man. Right then, let's fire away, shall we? Question number one. Where were you born?"

"In Malmesbury."

"When?"

"In 1925."

"Why?"

"To discover the purpose of existence."

"Aha. That gives us a bit of a line. Where did you go to school?"

"Golden Lodge Preparatory School."

"Did you like it?"

"No."

"Why not?"

"It wasn't likeable."

"Then where did you go?"

"Winchester."

"Were you happy there?"

"No."

"Why not?"

"It wasn't likeable."

"Did you ever wet your bed?"

"Once."

"Where?"

"In the Pay Corps."

"Did you get a commission?"

"No."

"Were you ever inordinately fond of the wicket-keeper?"

"No."

"Did you go to the university?"

"Yes, Cambridge."

"Were you happy there?"

"No."

"Why not?"

"I wanted to get out into the world."

"Did you?"

"Yes."

"Were you happy there?"

"No."

"Why not?"

"It wasn't a very nice world."

"Is abstract truth equatable with the ideals of the bourgeois?"

"No."

"Name your favourite English town."

This, Simpson reflected, was what W.O.S.B. must have been like.

"I haven't one."

"Name any English town."

"I can't decide which one to name."

"Name Kettering."

"Kettering."

"Who told you the facts of life?"

"The school doctor."

"What happened?"

"Wooldridge fainted."

"What profession did you take up when you left the university?"

"Seismography, catering, journalism, teaching, bus conducting, typing. . . ."

"What are you now?"

"Unemployed."

"Why did you leave all those jobs?"

"I was sacked. They weren't my vocation."

"What is?"

"I don't know yet."

"Ha ha ha, eh?"

"Yes."

"Well, that gives me quite a lot to be going on. Now let's turn to the events of the night of January 9th to 10th, shall we?" Much of the tension fell from the interrogation after this, since Simpson was so completely in the dark concerning the events of that night that it was not even necessary for him to be on his guard.

"So you remember nothing of the evening in question at all?" Ackroyd asked at length, after fruitlessly attempting for several minutes to extract some information on the subject.

"I'm afraid not."

"Have you seen a doctor recently?"

"Yes."

"What was wrong with you?"

"I don't know. The treatment was confidential."

"I see. Well, thank you, Mr Simpson. We'll have to see what we can do."

"Is there much hope?"

"It matters to you, does it?"

"Very much."

"Why?"

"I want to be free again."

"Why?"

"I want to discover the universal panacea for all mankind."

"I think there's hope. I'll work up a line of defence. I was interested in one or two things you said. Yes, I think there's hope. Soon have you nicely settled in one of those asylums. Ha ha ha, eh?"

14

DURING THE DAYS THAT FOLLOWED SIMPSON BEGAN to feel that they had better not concentrate too fully on the medical side. He would rather admit the whole thing, and more besides. Luckily nobody thought to charge him with anything else.

He began to have dreams of a world which was nothing but a vast asylum, in which there was nothing to do but sit on hard garden seats underneath yew trees or engage in interminable games of rehabilitative table tennis, which were always being interrupted by white-coated male nurses giving him his tea and rock cake at nineteen-all in the final set, so that nobody's cure would be impaired. One night they even had him painting daffodils. He would wake up from these dreams to find stretched around him the damp walls of his cell, which magnified a thousand times the restless creaking of his rude bed. Tiny drops of sweat gathered on his skin and as he sat up suddenly in his terror they poured down his chest and forehead and tickled the hollows of his body. Then he would gradually realise that this was only one of Her Majesty's prisons, and he was merely on remand. He would sink back onto his pillow then, in a travesty of relief, but the ache in his legs would not be relieved, and he would lie awake for the rest of the night, with the sweat drying cold on his body. Towards morning the relief would die away and the horror of the asylum would be as real to him in his wakefulness as it had been in his dreams.

During these long sleepless nights he would desperately attempt to concoct some alternative line of defence, which did not rely on the medical approach. But it was difficult, as difficult as it would have been for him to concoct a prosecution. It struck him that he at least was assured of a fair trial. Perhaps, he thought with a flicker of martyred relish, he was the first man ever to be given one. For it is only when neither side knows anything whatsoever about the alleged incidents that a trial can possibly be fair. In so many trials the facts incline towards the guilt or innocence of the accused party before the proceedings have even been opened. If trials were to be fair, let them be held before, rather than after, the offence with which they were concerned, he thought.

The calm which this thought engendered in him was abruptly shattered when he realised that there was no earthly reason, just because he knew nothing about the alleged incidents, why the prosecution should be equally ignorant. He was always the last to know about these things. Besides, as he saw now only too clearly, the fact that they were making allegations at all suggested that they had something up their sleeves. If they knew as little as he did they would be hard put to it to rustle up a prosecution. These thoughts caused Simpson renewed distress. When one party is in possession of the facts, and that party is not you, you have no chance whatever of a fair hearing. If there have to be facts at all, let them at least be shared equally among all the interested parties. He twisted his mind into agonies in his attempts to recall that fateful night, but all to no avail. It seemed impossible to defend

61

oneself unless one knew exactly what it was one had not done, and if one had not done it it was very difficult to know what it was.

The walls of the cell closed in on him during those days as if to press him like a fern. All over them little globules of sweat were spawning and constantly bursting, so that hundreds of tiny rivulets were forever running down the walls without managing to reach the floor.

Where had he been on the night in question? Could he perhaps have been mistaken for somebody else? Hardly. He was the sort of person who could easily be mistaken for absolutely anybody, and indeed almost always was. But people who can be mistaken for absolutely anybody are very rarely mistaken for anybody in particular. Then why could he remember nothing? Even if he had been completely drunk throughout the whole affair, he must have begun to get drunk somewhere, and he must have been in surroundings of some sort when he sobered up.

"Well, old boy, everything's going swimmingly," Ackroyd said to him one morning, on one of his regular but inconclusive visits. "There's no need to worry at all. The doc. says he's never seen a responsibility as diminished as yours. We'll get you fixed up somewhere where you'll be really well looked after. That'll be nice, won't it?"

"But I'm innocent," protested Simpson.

"Yes, yes. I know all about that. It's only natural."

"I'm innocent. If I only knew what had happened I could prove it."

"Of course you feel that way."

"I'll plead guilty."

"What?"

"I'll plead guilty."

"You can't do that, now we've got a defence."

"I'd rather plead guilty."

"But you said yourself that you were innocent."

"I don't want to go into an asylum."

And then poor, harrassed Ackroyd, his heartiness vanished, had to explain, all over again, Simpson's delusions. Of course he thought he was innocent. That was only to be expected. It is very hard to face up to the truth about oneself. But the fact that he wanted to plead guilty revealed, whatever explanations of it he might give, that on a subconscious level he was aware of his guilt. Of course it would be nice to spend a year or two in prison, and then be free. Everybody knew that. But what was nice wasn't always what was best for us. We couldn't always do what we wanted in this world. It was a pity, but there it was. That was what life was like. We had to accept it, whether we liked it or not. And we didn't always know ourselves what was best for us. Ackroyd always knew what was best for us. Ackroyd knew that it was his duty to see that Simpson was protected from society.

Simpson pointed out to him that in law a man is guilty until he is proved insane, but it was no use. Ackroyd's case was made up. They were dark days. The trial grew steadily nearer, and so settled was everything in Ackroyd's mind that he no longer even bothered to visit his client. Simpson was feeling at his lowest ebb, when, on the day before the trial, he had what was perhaps the first stroke of luck that he had ever enjoyed. A pleasant, un-assuming, friendly and gently-spoken man, with grey hair and lines on his forehead, appeared at the door, and announced that his name was Mr Burbage, and he was Simpson's new lawyer. Ackroyd, whose intention it was to visit connections in the tropics before the winter was out, had fallen seriously ill with anti-tetanus injections.

"I see that the defence is one of diminished responsibility," said Mr Burbage, having removed from his briefcase a bottle of claret and two glasses.

"A glass of wine?"

"Thank you."

Mr Burbage poured out the wine.

"I'm innocent."

"What?"

"It was Ackroyd's idea. He said he'd get me into an asylum."

"And you agreed?"

"I had no say in the matter."

"That's very bad."

"You mean I'll have a say with you?"

"I'm here to serve you."

"Thank you," said Simpson with definitive simplicity, and he smiled at Mr Burbage. A smile, which was shyly ashamed of being proud, jumped hastily from one of Mr Burbage's eyes to the other when it thought that no-one was looking. His little moustache seemed to come and go, and the lines on his forehead broke and dissolved like waves on a beach. A warm, inarticulate comradeship sparked in their bodies, a shared embarrassment that brought them closer together and made each wish that he was alone.

"Some more wine?" asked Mr Burbage.

"Thank you."

"What is your defence to these charges, then?"

"I know nothing about them."

"You weren't there?"

"I don't remember."

"But you don't believe you committed any offence?"

"I don't feel that I did."

"Good. Nice wine, isn't it?"

"Very."

"It's a pleasure to have an appreciative client. So many of one's clients are layabouts. Well, now, we haven't much time, Mr Simpson. The trial is tomorrow. I don't quite see what line we're to work on."

"No. What are we to say?"

"Well, we'll have to explain that you recall none of this whatsoever. So how could you have done it 'with intent'?"

"Will that work?"

"It's not brilliant, is it? But we have so little time, it's not easy. But we'll do our best."

"And if it's not enough?"

"I'm afraid you'll have a spell in prison."

"And then I'll be free?"

"Yes. I'm sorry. But it could be worse. A large number of my

64

clients like going to prison for short spells. We get people wanting to be purged, you know. But of course that doesn't apply to you. You're innocent."

"Yes."

"I'll do my best for you, Mr Simpson. That's all I can say."

"Thank you."

"I mean, we can't provide witnesses even."

"No."

"More wine?"

"Thank you."

"We're in a pickle."

"Your time's up," yelled the warder, bursting in on them.

"Oh, thank you. Well, I, I'll be off then. My time? I'm not a visitor. I'm his counsel."

"Oh, I'm sorry, sir. I thought you were a visitor." The warder cast a stern glance at the wine bottle, and departed. Mr Burbage smiled at Simpson.

"I know what you're thinking," he said, "but don't worry."

"What was I thinking?" asked Simpson, who had been thinking that he hadn't known he could have visitors.

"You're thinking that I don't seem very assertive. But please don't worry. I'm quite different in court. A lot of my clients get cold feet about me, but I'm afraid that's one of the penalties I pay for being what I am. I find it difficult to talk about myself, but you see – well, perhaps it's because I find it difficult to talk about myself. I'm a retiring person. But on the other hand, professionally, I find it quite easy to slip into the way of it. There are so many phrases that are helpful. My learned friend, and so on. Seeing my learned friend and knowing that I'm his learned friend, you know, I slip into my robes and I slip into the way of things. The arguments are interesting; I care for my clients, and that is what I think about. There's nothing personal involved. It must sound rather like a commercial, but I don't mean it that way. I'm trying to reassure you. Things are bound to be hard, but we won't do too badly. More wine?"

"Thank you."

There was a pause.

"I wasn't thinking that at all," said Simpson. "I was thinking that I hadn't known I could have visitors."

"You're allowed one visitor a week."

"This is a fine time to find out."

"They should have told you."

"It doesn't matter. I don't know. I don't know if she'd have come."

"I could arrange it, if you like."

"No."

"If you're sure. . . . Well, Mr Simpson, I must leave now. This has been a pleasure." He paused for a moment. "When all this business is over, I was wondering . . . I don't know if you're a drinking man."

"Not really. But one has to be sometimes."

"Exactly. Well, I was wondering, if you have nothing else to do, when all this business is over, if you'd care to come drinking with me one night."

"Yes, I would."

"I like an occasional night. It's quite nice at the Turton Arms. They have artists, but you don't have to listen to them."

"Yes, I'd like to."

"Well, I shall have to be off. I have another appointment, I'm afraid. I should like to have stayed. I've enjoyed it. But there it is. I'd better take the bottle and the glasses, I suppose. Thank you. Well, I'll have a look at the brief again tonight and check things over, and then I'll see you tomorrow."

"Yes."

"If you think of anything, telephone me. Oh, you can't, you're in prison. Damn. Well, never mind, we'll be able to talk before we get started tomorrow. Well, good-bye."

"Good-bye."

"I'm sorry to have to rush off like this."

"That's all right."

"Good-bye."

"Good-bye. Thank you for the wine."

"A pleasure. I like a good wine. Well, I'll see you at the trial. Do you know how to get there? Anyway, I expect they'll show you. Good-bye."

"Good-bye."

"Good-bye."

"Good-bye."

15

THE TRIAL WAS A BIG AFFAIR. THE ROOM WAS VERY full, and Simpson, who arrived late, was not given a very good seat. He glanced round the court. There was the judge with his wig and there were the counsel, whispering earnestly among themselves and passing each other important looking notes, and there was the clerk of the court, very lean and dry and very important, blowing his nose into his ledger and whispering earnestly to court officials, and there were the reporters, all with hangovers, frowning and scribbling and belching and whispering dirty stories, and there were the jury, eleven good men and one true woman, all whispering nervously and importantly among themselves and looking so isolated that it would have been no surprise if the foreman had suddenly run up a yellow flag. It was all very impressive, and Simpson, to whom nobody ever whispered anything, felt that he had no right to be there.

The case proceeded in a leisurely and inevitable way. Evidence was given, questions were asked and answered, examinations were made and crossed, and gradually, under the relentless questioning of Mr Leslie Walberswick, Q.C., the doleful happenings of the night of January 9 to 10 were revealed. They were much publicised in the newspapers of the time, but there was little that will go down in history. Mr Burbage did his best in defence, but he had little chance. There was tension, but it was of a slow and unexciting kind. The calm serenity of the court was disturbed only by one juryman, who, being allergic to oaths, entered upon a violent burst of sneezing as each new witness took the stand. Otherwise, most of the legal minds concerned took the opportunity of catching up on some badly needed sleep – there had been a Fancy Wig Ball the previous week – and woke up only to hear the summing up of Mr Justice Parkinson-Hoddinott.

"Lady and gentlemen of the jury," said Mr Justice Parkinson-Hoddinott, "You have heard the evidence that has been brought forward by both sides and you have seen, heard and smelt the various witnesses. You will have formed your own conclusions, and all twelve of you will have formed the same conclusion. If you have not already done so you will do so very shortly. It is not my task to put anything into your heads or to instruct you to return any particular verdict, although naturally I hope that you will. My function is simply to direct you on certain matters, and to see that justice is, or is not, done, according to the verdict that you return today.

"In considering your verdict you will have to consider in turn each of four charges, and in the case of each charge you must ask yourselves: 'Is the accused guilty or not guilty?' Your verdict will depend upon your answer to that question, and your answer to that question will depend upon whether you are satisfied that it has been proved by the prosecution beyond reasonable doubt that the accused committed the offence with which he is charged.

"You have heard the case for the prosecution. On the first charge, that of uttering obscene documents and melodies, several witnesses – and the court is most grateful to them for allowing themselves to be grabbed by the police, and dragged here today in Black Marias – have told you that they heard the accused singing obscene parodies of Dutch hymns outside the Grease and Axle Tavern in Corporation Street on the night of January 9 to 10. You may be satisfied, from the descriptions given, that these were obscene melodies, and when I tell you that in law a melody, and indeed practically anything else, is often referred to as a document, you may feel satisfied that this charge has been proved. That is entirely up to you.

"Other witnesses, to whom we are no less indebted, have described the accused's behaviour towards his wife, and she in court has related more than thirty acts of cruelty committed by him. The defence, in its turn, has asked for a watering can to be taken into account. Today you are concerned with only one of these acts, that of wilfully and with malice aforethought parking his wife upon a bombed site. Witnesses have told you that this good lady was found, securely roped to the foundations of a ruined department store with rope bought by the accused that very afternoon. You may think that this is sufficient to prove that he was wilful and had malicious aforethoughts. That is a matter for you to decide.

"You have also heard the evidence of another lady, a most material witness. This lady, Mrs Gertrude Walsh, who has been described here today as a lady of the very highest motives, has related the manner in which she was kidnapped, and she has told you that in her opinion – and you will bear in mind, when you decide that it is almost certainly the truth, that it was only an opinion – it was with intent. Several independent witnesses have corroborated her evidence of sudden abduction in a light goods van, and have given the opinion that it was with intent. One witness, a highly respected hairdresser, of impeccable reputation, has told you: 'There could have been no other motive.' You may feel that under the circumstances the charge has been proved – or you may not.

"We come now to the charge of conduct liable to cause a breach of promise. It is a shocking tale that has been unfolded in this court during these last few days. You may feel, you are of course completely at liberty to feel, lady and gentlemen, that such conduct is fast becoming normal in this age of coca-cola, flick knives, drug addicts and pop records. On the other hand a parson has told you that he believes such conduct to constitute a breach not only of promise but also of probation, common decency and the peace. 'One long breach from start to finish' was how he described the incidents, but of course you may feel that he is not 'a with it hep cat.' That is a matter that each of you, searching your own conscience, will have to weigh for yourselves.

"You are of course at liberty to decide that all these people, who have unblemished records and gave their evidence under oath, were lying. That is entirely a matter for you. But if you feel that they, or even some of them, are telling the truth – and no doubt you will pay proper attention to the fact that their statements, taken by several different officers, and their evidence before this court tally in every single particular – then you have no alternative but to return a verdict of guilty.

"You have also heard the case for the defence. The defence have based their case upon a plea of not guilty and have asked that it be taken into account. I hope that it will be, but I venture to suggest that it does not, in itself, constitute an adequate explanation. Indeed the most significant feature of the defence seems to me, just as it will in a few minutes seem to you, to be that no explanation of these occurrences has been put forward. Yet they occurred. The defence has pointed out that the accused has absolutely no recollection of that night, and that surely such activities as kidnapping with intent, which a man does not do every day, would have stuck in his mind. To which one is entitled to ask: 'What man?' Most men, it is true, do not kidnap with intent every day. This man, perhaps, does. We do not know. We must discount this consideration. If this man can provide no explanation, and yet it is said that he did these things, and you accept that evidence, and I have outlined to you how reliable this evidence appears, on the face of it, to be, and if you accept the defendant's profession that he knows nothing of these matters, bearing in mind that no doubt has been cast upon this profession by the prosecution, then you will I think be forced to conclude that he must have been drunk or drugged or that he is suffering from amnesia. Now a man does strange things when he is drunk. He may do them with strange intent, even with drunken intent, but none the less with intent. A man who suffers from amnesia nevertheless did those things that he did, and his intent was no less strong because he cannot recall it now. Ignorance is no excuse in law. The defence have asked you to take a good look at Mrs Walsh and consider whether an action of the kind alleged could possibly be taken against her with intent. You may think that this is an unwarranted comment upon a lady whose misfortune it is to be revoltingly ugly. You may also feel that this question serves only to obscure the real question: 'Did this man do these things?', since I think I have shown you that, however improbable the intent, it was intent if this man did these things. If therefore you believe that the whole defence has been merely a specious legal quibble, at a time when we are dealing with the kind of crime that threatens the safety of our whole civilisation, then you have no alternative but to return a verdict of guilty. If, however, you incline to the view that the defence has made a conscientious attempt to arrive at the truth in this matter, you will probably find this attempt pathetically inadequate. That, however, is a matter on which you, and you alone, have the final say.

"In considering your verdict, lady and gentlemen of the jury, do not allow personal considerations to influence you. You must not be weighed by prejudice or ill-will, by fear or favour, nor must you allow your hearts to rule your heads. Do not be lenient to this man out of pity, or severe out of contempt, just because he happens to be an example of humanity at its most abject.

"Do not, in the name of our great system of English law, listen to your emotions. Do not be swayed, gentlemen, by the fact that it could have been your wife who was so savagely and without reason parked on a bombed site on a bitterly cold January night. Ignore, lady, that it might have been your husband who left you to suffer the rigours of cold and desolation. Forget that the Dutch, extracts from whose hymns you have heard parodied in court, are not some primitive tribe of marauding barbarians, whose superstitious and ill-conceived chants we may feel at liberty to mock, but a tiny, brave, seafaring, flower-loving Christian nation, who fought, and suffered alongside us, in the most cataclysmal Armaggedon in the whole history of human kind."

Simpson was found guilty of all four charges. He was sent to prison for twelve months, with six weeks costs.

16

SIMPSON WAS ESCORTED TO HIS CELL BY TWO VAST, cheerless warders who kicked him every few yards and then glared malevolently at him when he did not become violent. It was as if they were making tiny little chips at the great rock of violence which was embedded in their hearts. He felt sorry for them, but once inside his cell and left entirely alone he soon began to feel sorry for himself. He was cold, hungry and bruised, and the time that he had to serve lay heavily upon him.

For many long hours during the days and nights that followed he reflected bitterly on the history of disasters that had been his life. What had he done that had brought him to such a situation? Here he was, five foot ten in his socks, and they were extremely thick socks—that was about the only compensation of prison life. Here he was, some eleven and a half stone, with a second class degree and receding hair, imprisoned in a tiny bare cell which, however ingeniously he might measure it, remained unbearably small. Here he was, approaching his fortieth birthday, still searching for the purpose of existence, and they had compelled him to spend the best part of a year, even allowing for any possible remission, in this confinement, while less than three miles away Mrs Pollard kept his room empty, or did not, in case he should, or shouldn't, return. He wanted desperately, in those early days, to know whether his room was being kept empty or not, and he had visions of it in which it was empty, just as he had left it, and visions, horrible vivid visions, in which a flamboyantly moustachioed upstart was occupying it and had filled it with his big-game hunting trophies. The food was bad, and often in those early days he would not eat it, and a warder would kick him. His ankles swelled badly, and a doctor was summoned. He refused to believe Simpson's story and diagnosed damp. Cognate failure of the lobes, he called it, and when Simpson suggested that ankles have no lobes the doctor gave him a sharp kick on the right knee which incapacitated him completely for several days. What could he have done to deserve such treatment?

Bit by bit he began to remember. It was dark. Yes, dark. Extraordinarily dark. He was singing. The song was Dutch. Where could he possibly have picked up a song like that? That he could not recall. But evidently he had, on some youthful carouse, and it had stuck. One read of old ladies who recited vast stretches of the Koran on their death bed, not having been in contact with it for nigh on seventy years. And here he was, singing this wretched song in Corporation Street. What a place to be in at that time of night. The road was up, and he kept stumbling against the high wall which ran beside the railway. The wind was cold, and a few flurries of snow froze on his face. Somewhere to the left a woman laughed harshly. The laugh rang out very clear on the cold air, and then he recalled no more.

And so, very gradually, in the middle distance of his head, he began to remember. But married? Him, married? That was the rock on which his memories broke in vain. Many years ago there had almost been a Miss Wilkinson. A few weeks ago there had been times when he thought there might be a Mrs Pollard, if he wasn't careful. In between there had been no question of there being anybody. He had never come anywhere near to being married. Nowhere near it. And now they came along with this woman, this Esme Simpson. They exhibited her before him in court, and he felt no flicker of recognition. If he had married her it must have caused some violent reaction in him, for him to forget it like this. But then something pretty violent must have been necessary to get him married in the first place, so alien to his life did it seem. So perhaps it was not surprising that he should recall none of it, and that it should have ended in such complete estrangement.

Nevertheless it was necessary for him to try and recall it, if he was to come to terms with his situation. And in the end he did. Had they been married in a registry office? Had they tied an old boot to her bottom? He seemed to recall something of the sort. It was vague, and it comforted him, but it led to further memories that were not vague, and did not comfort him. Failures, inadequacies, arguments and moments of bitter silence. Disgust, nausea, and a desire for unattainable freedom. Petty, mortifying scenes. He recalled insults that had been hurled at him, to which there had been no reply. And he recalled the final squabble.

There had been some trouble on a bombed site, some sort of scuffle. Esme was sitting on an old block of stone and shouting at him. Someone swore and threw a stone. It rang out against a tin as it fell. The ripple of sound fanned out through the silence, and in the silence, somewhere to the left, a woman laughed harshly. The laugh rang out very clear on the cold night air. Gertrude Walsh!

So that was what he had done. He had wilfully, maliciously and without authority uttered obscene documents and melodies. He had wilfully and with malice aforethought parked his wife, Esme Simpson, upon a bombed site, contrary to the Spouse Protection Act of 1623. He had wilfully and maliciously kidnapped with intent one Gertrude Walsh – and no man would ever kidnap two Gertrude Walshes. He had behaved throughout the whole ghastly business in a manner liable to cause a breach of promise.

We all have a great deal to learn about ourselves, and the process is often a difficult one, but Simpson had more to learn about himself than anyone, and for him the process was particularly difficult. His whole upbringing, from the name tapes to the battle of Trafalgar, had fostered the belief that he was "all right really". Timid and feeble he might be, frightened of rugger he undoubtedly was, but he wasn't completely bad. He wasn't a Frenchman or a gypsy or anything like that. And he had a knowledge of himself too – a knowledge uniquely his – a sight of a beautiful soul that nobody else could see. Now, for the first time all this was in doubt. Now, for the first time, he had to face up to the possibility that he was bad, utterly bad.

His immediate reaction was a grotesque shame, shame not at what he had done, not at anything Mrs Pollard might think when she found out about it all, but shame that he had let Mr Anning down. Every week in the scouts – where he had not stayed long, having been an abysmal failure, and utterly miserable – they had each done, or tried to do, a good turn. The only week when they did not do a good turn was Bob-A-Job Week, when turns cost money. Every other week they tried to do a good turn, and one week they had all been out in the woods, baking potatoes in their jackets on a boiling hot day and generally having wonderful fun, and Millington's potato had got burnt to a cinder, and Millington had blubbered. He gave his potato to Millington, as his good turn, and Millington gave it back to him, as his good turn, and Mr Anning, laying a firm hand on their shoulders, had said, as his good turn: "I'm proud of you both." Words had stuck in their throats then. What would Mr Anning say about this? What would Millington, doubtless a bishop by now, say? The absurd shame welled up inside him, and the nearest he could get to ridiculing himself for it was a sad little smile to the walls of his cell.

After a while the shame began to give way before a slow trickle of guilt. The guilt began to grow into a flood, and with it came joy. He would mortify himself, and if he didn't the warders would do it for him. Then he would be purged, he would be renewed, his soul would be beautiful again, deep down.

It was at this moment that he was given the special privilege of being transferred to Renstock Model Prison, on the South Downs. Here they gave him things to do – books to read, tasks to perform, social activities to engage in. He was encouraged to do some painting. He was allowed to wander in the charming grounds in which the light, airy Scandinavian-style buildings were discreetly, even elegantly, set. He was taken to the prison's accommodation agency, "Share A Cell Ltd.", and encouraged to answer questions about his habits and hobbies, so that he could share his rehabilitation with suitable companions, and the benevolent organisers were livid when he explained that he wanted to be on his own. They made him share a hut with a literary counterfeit expert and with Millington, who had been living off the earnings of prostitution. He had virtually none of the discomforts and absolutely none of the privacy which were essential if he was to achieve any real success. The days passed in an appalling atmosphere of synthetic good-will and Simpson, at his lowest ebb, took no interest in the varied and thoroughly regenerative meals provided by the prison's progressive dietician or in the series of lovely sunsets which hung over the Sussex downs each evening.

One day, when he was judged to have fully settled in, he was summoned for an interview with the Governor.

"You've had a chance to settle in here, Simpson," said the Governor.

"Yes, sir."

"Ever done any acting?"

"No, sir."

"Good. Be all the more effective. Take you out of yourself."

"That's just what I . . ."

"I know what you're going to say. Well, you're quite right. But in acting the part of someone else you find yourself. We do a little play every three months. We've just done *Hamlet*. Not a great success. Ophelia got a remission for good conduct on the day of the dress rehearsal. The chaplain did a rush job on the play, rewrote it without her in it, but it wasn't the same. Our next play is to be *Dear Octopus*. Not ideal for an all-male cast, perhaps, but . . ."

"I don't want to act, sir."

"It's the things that we don't want to do that it is often best for us to do. Man is his own worst doctor."

"It won't help me to act, sir."

"We want you to feel part of the community here, Simpson. We want to make you feel wanted."

"I am wanted here. But I don't want to be here, sir."

"Don't you like my prison?"

76

"It's very nice."

"Scandinavian style."

"It's very nice, sir. But I . . . I want to go back."

"You must serve your sentence."

"I want to go back to the other prison."

"What?"

"I have done wrong. I want to pay for it."

"We must all pay for our sins."

"I want to suffer."

"Real suffering is the suffering you don't choose, Simpson. If you really want to suffer we can arrange it here."

The Governor was as good as his word. Simpson was co-erced into every progressive, regenerative and rehabilitative scheme in the place, with disastrous effect. It was not that he attempted to sabotage these schemes. It was just that his complete lack of enthusiasm slowly pervaded his colleagues. *Dear Octopus* was even more of a disaster than *Hamlet*, the meetings of the Friends of Iago drew record low attendances, and a reading of *Paradise Lost* developed into the first riot ever to occur in a progressive British prison. It was not much of a riot, in fact, it was little more than a high-spirited expression of boredom, but by the time a con-man who was serving a five-year sentence crept out at dead of night and telephoned it to every paper in Fleet Street it was very much of a riot. The Governor was on the carpet, but he felt that if he had a scapegoat he might be able to get at least one foot off the carpet. Simpson was always the first goat to be scaped in any gathering, and often with a good deal less justice than on this occasion, so that it was no surprise to him when he got his wish and found himself all alone again in his dark, dripping cell.

Six months of his sentence still remained, and at first he enjoyed his mortification. Life in prison had a steady routine which pleased him, and interruptions were few. Three times a day, at 7.22, 1.16 and 6.58, a man brought him a meal of bread and stew, which he watered down with a chipped brown mug of hot buttered tea. He was a big man, and he had, as was only fair, a big face, this man who brought him his meals. Sometimes he smiled and sometimes he frowned, and every now and then he delivered a hearty kick. Usually he smiled. On the 10th he smiled three times. On the 11th he frowned at 7.22 and 1.16, but at 6.58 he smiled. On the 12th he smiled three times and at 1.16 he delivered a hearty kick. That was about his norm.

On Mondays they brought him a silver trolley known as "The Library." On it there were a number of Bibles and old-fashioned novels, and one or two pamphlets with titles like: *How to make your spare time essential, Thirty decorative uses for tin foil, The fight against Metropolitan crime* and *Family Planning – Is it man's Waterloo?* He was allowed one novel and one Bible every week, but after the first week he only bothered with the novel, as he found that the plots of the Bibles were all the same.

Once a week the chaplain visited him. He was a tall man with round shoulders and a convex face, and when he laughed his eyes seemed totally impervious to the merriment that was going on all round them. Simpson did not like him. These visits apart, he had himself to himself. Once a day he had to walk round the courtyard in his underclothes – a whim of the Governor, who believed in physical fitness – and from time to time he would be asked to make a bucket or two. This he quite enjoyed. The mechanical activity gave his mind ever greater freedom in which to enjoy his mortification.

Gradually, however, a dreadful thing began to happen. He became bored with his mortification, and even grew to hate it. He had had quite adequate guilt feelings, felt thoroughly purged, and yet had made no progress whatever towards the universal panacea for all mankind. This search into himself, he was beginning to realise, was not at all the way in which to find it. It could only be found through action, and action which involved relationships with other people, of that he became convinced. And once he knew that he grew impatient to be out. The days began to seem interminable, and now there was no consolation to be had. Even his buckets were not a success, springing mysterious leaks after a few hours. His morale became extremely low, and had he not caught double pneumonia as a result of walking round the courtyard in his underclothes it is doubtful whether he could have borne those last months. To give way to illness was a luxury, and by the time he was sufficiently recovered to regain his full identity not more than two months of his captivity remained.

These months he spent groaning, and eating, and even once or twice beating his head against the walls. Often he would think of Mrs Pollard, and wonder what, if anything, had become of her. Why had she not come to see him? Even now, as he thought of her, she was somewhere, she was occupying a given moment in time and space, the same moment in time as him, but an utterly different space, where she was actually engaged on some activity, however trivial. She could at least have thought of leaving it for a while and visiting him. He wondered whether she even knew what had happened to him, whether she had made any enquiries, whether she cared.

If only she was still alive, he felt sure that he could win her. It was what he wanted, he felt sure of that now, and he had the added spur of knowing that it was in relationships of that kind that the panacea was to be sought. He would adopt an entirely new policy towards her and sweep her off her feet, so long as she was still alive.

Awake. Asleep. Awake. Asleep. Eating. Not eating. So it went on, and the days passed. At first the passing of the days afforded a slight relief to his pain, but gradually, as only a month, then three weeks, then a fortnight remained, the greater his agony became. The period between 7.22 and 1.16, and between 1.16 and 6.58, grew longer and longer, and the uneasy half-world between sleep and wakefulness which stretched from 6.58 until 7.22 the next morning was a continuous nightmare. By the time only one day remained the tension had become so great that he felt that he could bear it no longer, that it would be impossible for him to survive for twenty four more hours. And a new fear came over him, a fear that he would do something dreadful before the day was out, and would lose his remission for good conduct.

Twenty-three hours. Twenty-two. Twenty-one. The pressure had grown no greater, and he began to feel that he would pull through. Twenty. Nineteen. Eighteen. He was certain of it. A sudden lightness entered his body, and for a few seconds he felt astonishingly peaceful and astonishingly powerful. Then the joy was gone, and he no longer cared. There was no desire any more, just flatness, as far as the mind could see.

The night came, and he slept. The dawn came, and he awoke. The day came, and he ate the breakfast that was put before him. He allowed himself to be given his possessions. He changed into his clothes, though he no longer recognised them as his own. He was led down a long stone corridor, and at the end there was a door. The door was opened, and he found himself in the street. The door was closed behind him. The sun was shining brightly on the frozen snow.

17

THERE, WAITING OUTSIDE A NEWSAGENT'S, WAS MR Burbage. He came forward with a delighted smile on his face and they shook hands.

"Well," said Mr Burbage. "You haven't forgotten, have you? You're coming drinking with me tonight, at the Turton Arms, to celebrate. There'll be artists, but we needn't listen to them."

Simpson did not care whether he went to the Turton Arms or not, so he said: "Right."

"You didn't think I'd forget, did you?"

"No."

"I found out the day of your release from the Governor. What's the trouble? The sun a bit bright for you?"

"Er – yes."

"It must be a bit of a change. Shall we go for some coffee? I know a place."

"All right."

They entered a coffee establishment known to Mr Burbage.

"I hope you didn't feel we did too badly at the trial," said Mr Burbage, twisting his spoon in his hand.

"No."

"How did they treat you? All right?"

"Yes."

"Well I daresay you feel a bit funny still. I'll expect to hear all about it later on."

After coffee it was nearly time to have lunch, so they went to a pub and nearly had lunch. Then they went to the Cartwright Grill and had lunch. Simpson had very little to say, but Mr Burbage seemed to understand and they sat in restful silence for much of the time, with Mr Burbage occasionally giving a brief description of some of his more interesting cases.

After lunch Mr Burbage said that he had a few routine matters to see to at the office. Perhaps Simpson wanted to go home and change and wash. Simpson did not. For the first time since leaving prison he felt a reaction, and he explained to Mr Burbage that once he had gone back home he would find it difficult to get out for the evening. His landlady, Mr Burbage would understand. The motherly type. Mr Burbage did understand, and Simpson went to the cinema. It was warm in the cinema and he felt lulled by the noise. The programme was a bit trying at first but after he had seen it through once he felt that it would be nice to see it again, now that he need feel no anxiety over what was going to happen, and he was sorry when the time came to leave. It was dark and the wind was extremely cold, and it was difficult to leave the warm protection of the cinema and strike off up the bustling street.

He met Mr Burbage as arranged, and they caught a crowded bus which led them high up past the city waterworks, through sooty stone suburbs, until it reached an enormous cross-roads. There, black and aggressive, stood the squat, square building of the Turton Arms.

"It's my local," said Mr Burbage apologetically. "It's nicer inside."

They went inside. The pub was large and almost empty, except for a few people huddled against the bar. It would not fill up until after eight o'clock. Until then there would not be very much atmosphere, and Simpson found it difficult to abandon himself. He was thinking about his wife. Didn't one have to make settlements on people of that sort? That would be an obstacle to his hopes of finding the universal . . .

The panacea! Of course! That was what he was for. It was a long time now since he had thought of the panacea. Too long.

"Drink up."

He drank up. The beer was good.

"Same again?"

"Thanks."

"Good, isn't it?"

"Yes."

"They keep it well here."

"Yes."

Mr Burbage went to the bar and bought two drinks. The industrial golfers who were leaning against the counter looked at him as if he was something the cat had brought in and would presently take out again. Then they returned to their drinks. Mr Burbage brought the drinks back to Simpson and said apologetically: "It gets livelier later on."

Simpson experienced a return of the warmth he had felt for Mr Burbage in prison, and he said: "It's all right in here." Then they drank their drinks and Mr Burbage said: "Same again?" and Simpson said: "Thanks", and Mr Burbage went to the bar and bought two more drinks. This time the industrial golfers did not even bother to look at him, and quite soon he brought the drinks back to their table. He said: "You'll feel better when you have some more beer inside you," and Simpson said: "Yes," and Mr Burbage said: "It takes a bit of getting used to, being free again."

Then Simpson said he was sorry that he had no money and asked him if he was sure he didn't mind paying for all the drinks, and Mr Burbage explained that he had no one else to spend his money on.

Then they drank.

Then Mr Burbage said: "Ever thought of going into business?"

"No," said Simpson.

Then they drank.

Then Mr Burbage sought his advice about the new wallpaper for his bachelor flat. It had resolved into a choice between light grey, and Simpson agreed that it was an excellent choice. Mr Burbage told him of all the plans he had for the rejuvenation of his flat. Simpson wanted to tell of his plans. He wanted very much to confide in this new friend of his and win his approval. Somehow, however, each time he was on the verge of beginning, he hesitated. Eventually, after several minutes of misery, he decided to keep them to himself until he could present them as a *fait accompli*. It was wiser that way.

"Drink up," said Mr Burbage, noting his unease.

"I'm sorry. I'm not used to drink."

"Anyway, you've someone to look after you."

That was true. And he owed it to Mr Burbage. He drank up. That was it. That was the way to live. Swing the glass, swing.

Mr Burbage went to the bar and bought two more drinks. Then he returned.

"I enjoy drinking with you."

"So do I."

Which of them was speaking? Or had their personalities already merged? Did not everything begin to merge? Did not the walls and the gathering smoke and the filling, clinking room and the talking and the shadows and the walnut and the irises of their lovely eyes merge? Mr Burbage was talking. He'd better listen.

They talked of the Devon coast, and many other things, and to Simpson it was as if neither of them was there any more.

"I know that man," said Mr Burbage suddenly. "Schoolmaster. Nice chap. He lives in my road. He doesn't get out very often. I'll fetch him over."

He went over to the bar to fetch the schoolmaster, but he returned alone. "Pity," he said. "He has some pupils to discuss. You'd have liked him. A nice, quiet chap."

Mr Burbage bought two more drinks. As they drank them he began to talk about his childhood, when the days had been long and the summers had been hot and long, hot loaves of fresh bread had stood on the low, wooden table in the scullery. The little boy Burbage was still wearing short trousers then, and his legs were not yet something to be ashamed of, but he was old enough to listen while his grandfather sat by the window, gazing out over the hollihocks that stretched towards the orchard, and told him how his grandfather had loved to sit there by the old reddened wall of the orchard and talk to him about his youth. In those days jugs of fresh, warm milk had stood on the table in the scullery and his grandfather had loved to take him to the old mill and tell him how he had stood with his grandfather, listening to the roar of the water as it came through the floury old mill and set off on its long, brave journey to Holland. All the little boy could see was a clear, minnowy stream with a lot of nettles on its hot banks, but he liked to hear how the water grew swollen and muddy and travelled all the way across the sea to Holland. His grandfather had told him that when he grew up he must work hard. Great new times were coming, and if he worked hard there would be no limit to what he could do. He had worked hard, the great new times had come and gone, and he had told his grandson that he must work hard, because great new times were coming. He had told his grandson that he must work hard, because great new times were coming. The great new times had come and gone, he had worked hard, and he had told his grandson that he must work hard, because great new times were coming. He had worked hard, the great new times had come and gone, and he had told his grandson to work hard, because great new times were coming.

"I have worked hard," said Mr Burbage, and then he told how the house had been sold to a Major-General, who had converted the orchard into an Eton fives court.

Then he said: "Same again?" and Simpson said: "Thanks,"

and Mr Burbage bought two more drinks. Then they drank.

Did not Mrs Pollard merge? Mrs Pollard and the irises of her bathroom taps and the clinking filling of her teeth, and the onion and the carrot and did not Miss Daisy Wilkinson merge? He drank up, and they merged. That was the way. Swing the glass, swing. Soon be there. Panacea. Very exclusive club. For all mankind. Nobody else admitted in any circumstances unless in evening dress. He felt sure that he had lost something, or had forgotten something. Never mind, he must drink up. That was the important thing. See, he has raised his glass and is drinking.

"There's a chap I'd like you to meet. Odd fish altogether, but I think you'll find him interesting. Hey there, Setters."

"Dear Mr Burbage, I do like his little moustache," thought Simpson.

"He used to be a Major-General. Now he's a journalist of some sort. He does a lot of literary criticism. He'd do quite well if he moved to London, but he won't. He has an inferiority complex."

Eventually Mr Burbage managed to drag Setters over. He was a drinking man, big and red. Introductions were effected. Then some more beer went down and there was talk. Simpson, much to his amazement, made some polite enquiries.

"I had to leave the army on account of this game leg," said Setters in answer to one of them.

"He isn't interested in your leg," said Mr Burbage.

"I am," said Simpson.

"I'll show it to you some time."

"He doesn't want to see your leg. He's just come out of prison."

"I'd like to see it."

"Prison, eh?"

"I want to see it very much."

"I'll show it to you in the gents, if you like."

"I want you two to get together and talk literature," said Mr Burbage.

"Are you a literary man?" enquired Setters.

Simpson blushed. "I used to write poems."

"Good man."

"You must show them to Setters. He'll criticise them for you."

"Healthy criticism never did anyone any harm."

"He'll bring them as soon as he can."

"I've thrown them all away."

"Thrown them away? Why?"

"They weren't any good."

"That's the spirit. I always wanted to be a poet. Never really had the gift of the gab, though. That's what it is, you know. A gift. A knack."

"Yes," Simpson murmured, twisting his glass uneasily.

"Setters commanded a division during the war, didn't you?"

"Yes I did, come to mention it. What did you do?"

"I was in the Pay Corps for the last two years."

"And before that?" barked Setters.

"Before that I was too young," said Simpson politely.

"Disgraceful. What would Kipling have said if he'd heard you say a thing like that? Anyway, as I was saying, I hadn't got the flair or whatever it is for poetry, so I went into the army. Only thing to do, eh? Well, soldiering is soldiering and literature is literature. Then I got this blasted leg – I'll show it to you in a minute – and I gave up soldiering and went back to literature. Cut your coat to suit your cloth. I mean, a soldier, he volunteers for a dangerous assignment, they ask 'How many legs has he got?' It counts against you. I must say I've never really regretted it, though. Your soldier, he may win wars, but your critic, he criticises literature."

'Once in a train, a long time ago,' thought Simpson, 'I did . . . nothing. Once upon a time I must have married Mrs Simpson. What's the stupid drunk saying?'

". . . spread literary values a bit. I think I may be said to have an open mind, but I'm damned if I call that coffee bar stuff art. Some of those young nappy slappers, I'd like to get them in uniform. Greek art, that was the stuff. They may not have known how to treat their women but they had some great art. Just a bull on a vase, and there it is. Greatness."

"I'm sure you agree with that," said Mr Burbage, and he called to a waiter – there were waiters after 8.30, obsequious in their white coats – and ordered three more drinks. It made him feel good, managing to catch the waiter's eye so quickly.

"Aeschylus, an artist. Aristophanes, an artist. There was some backbone to it. It had something. It was manly. I may only have been a soldier, but I think I know great art when I see it."

Purged, thought Simpson. A new life. No more words. Actions. When his glass arrived he banged it martially on the table. It broke, and the beer foamed all over his trousers. Never mind. Over there, by the bar, with her hair undone, sat universal love. Smoky and dusky like a potato in its jacket she was steaming over there by the bar with her hair undone and her lips done in a pout. Over there he would go. A new life. Any second now he would feel his feet rise and he would walk over to her and tell her that she had been chosen.

The dogs. On all sides the thirsty hounds were baying. What on earth did they find to bay to each other? Leave her for the moment. The universal panacea would still be there in the morning. Tonight, life. It was easier. Life, a babble of consuming tongues.

"Sixteen overs an hour! They'd never have stood for it between the wars."

"Did you hear the one about the Ethiopian tent maker?"

"I think he was Irish. Nice, though."

"Didn't know old Parsons had it in him."

"Very cold."

"Snowing when I left home."

"In broad daylight, right outside Marks and Spencers."

"So he lifted up the flap of the third tent, and there was another beautiful . . ."

No, thought Simpson. He had better find the universal panacea pretty soon. There was no time to lose.

Over there by the bar universal love was smiling, and for a moment he thought she was smiling at him, but no, she was smiling at a big hooked nose, hooked to a big accountant, who was counting his blessings as he spoke to her with her potatoes in her jacket and her hair over there by the bar. Oh well, let the accountant reach out to the new life, if that was fate. Too tired now. No time. Later. Must drink up. Down in the sediment resides the ultimate. See it, the lees. There would be silence at the bottom of the glass.

He reached the bottom of the glass, and damn it, the man was still talking. What a bore! And he was talking to him!

"You're an educated man," he was saying. "Cambridge and Winchester. Excellent names. Excellent names. You can't go far wrong with names like that. I went to Sandhurst myself. Sandhurst sir. Excellent for a soldier, no damned good for a literary critic. No books. Rifles. But I learnt a thing at Sandhurst. You want to know what it was, don't you?"

"No."

"Discipline. I may not be a great intellectual, but I think I can recognise discipline when I see it. A beginning, a middle and an end."

Some of them were going round in circles and others were going round in straight lines and he was going round and over there by the bar she was going round. In a minute he would go over to her and tell her that he loved her and that he held the key to her future happiness. Not yet, though. He had better wait until she had stopped going round in circles. Some people didn't like being interrupted when they were going round in circles.

Suddenly, just when he was about to walk boldly up to her and confess that it would be impossible for him to live without her and he would always hold her in the deepest affliction, she stopped going round in circles, stood up, and put her arm round the accountant's waist. They minced happily from the room, to do their audits, doubtless. Simpson stirred uneasily, like a peat bog, with his vocation shattered by a cruel blow of fate. Then, with a brilliant inspiration, he felt hungry.

"I say," he blurted out. "Where are the goodies?"

Mr Burbage smiled approvingly at this and he went to the bar and bought some crisps and cheese straws and three more drinks. Simpson sat, with a new contentment, munching his crisps.

"I like a poem to show some discipline," said Setters.

"Get your head down, Wordsworth," shouted Simpson so loudly that several people actually turned to look and listen. "Come on now, get your dressing, you hexameters. In line now. Careful, Byron, those aren't blanks, you know. Oh, naughty Byron. You've shot Keats. Tut tut. That wasn't a very sensible thing to do now, was it? You were supposed to be on the same side. Have you polished your style this morning, Samuel Taylor?"

"I'm sorry," said Mr Burbage anxiously to Setters. "He's been in prison, you know."

"I can't say I'm altogether surprised," said Setters. "You long-haired wierdies can't fool me just by wearing a convict crop. I wish you'd been in my division. Well, old boy, I'll be pushing along."

"Yes. Good-bye. I'm sorry about this."

"Not your fault. You get them."

Drink up. As a man increases in stature, so does he drink up. And as he drinks up he approaches nearer to the attainment of his aims in life.

"Did I upset him?" Simpson asked.

"I'm afraid so," said Mr Burbage, with a forgiving smile.

"Good. I'm glad. Nothing but trenches from the moment he came in."

Were these the artists? Was this the turn? A stir of boredom ran through the assembly. Three seedy men slithered onto the platform, clicking everything that could be clicked, smiling with everything that could be smiled with. The Three Penfolds.

As they sang Simpson's universal love was stirring. It was as if he was trying to burst into leaf. But he was too old. He was a dead old tree which grew where there had only been mud and where there would only be mud again. He was strong and gnarled and around his mossy bole the fog swirled. Through the fog a blackboard swirled. It was long ago, at school, in the labs.

On Doctor Finney's blackboard there had been a man and there had also been a woman. Wooldridge had fainted. Long ago there had been mud and dinosaurs in the labs at school. They had come far, those early Druid children, to learn to distinguish the dinosaur from the pterodactyl, to learn to wear long trousers.

It was foggy. Nearer at hand there was a woman, but this was not his woman, so there were two women, and, if there were two women, which of them was universal, and, if not, where was Mrs Pollard and why didn't he drink up?

"I'm universal man," he shouted.

"Quiet."

"Bloody hell, isn't anybody interested? I should have thought it was worth listening to. Perhaps you didn't hear what I said. I said: 'I'm universal man.'"

"Quiet. You'll have us thrown out."

Who was this idiot? Oh, it was Burbage. Nice old Burbage. It was nice to lie in the mud alongside Burbage, the one coniferous, the other deodorant, with their fat, knotted trunks sinking slowly into the primeval slime, where below the mossy earth they would merge. I, thou, he she or it, we, you (plural), they merge, and still half a glass to drink. Drink up.

"I could have," said Simpson dogmatically.

"Could have what?"

"Anything. I distinctly recall her. I – I never meant to do it. Or not to. You understand that, don't you, Georgie?"

"Yes."

"Good ole Georgie. You're a good chap, Georgie. You may only be a commissionaire or whatever it is you are, but I'll say this for you, Garbage old man, you're my mate." His head nodded against the table. He let it lie on his cheek and he squinted up at Mr Burbage with bloodshot eyes.

"You'll come with me on bob-a-job week, won't you, Georgie?" he asked.

"Yes. Of course I will."

"Good old Georgie." He pointed his forefinger very seriously at Mr Burbage. "Tell me, Garbage old man," he said. "You're a

90

man of the world, aren't you? I thought you were. Tell me, Garbage, this love, and all that stuff, it's pretty important, isn't it? Because bloody hell, I – listen, Garbage. I'm going to tell you something. I – I wannago."

And his head fell down in the midst of all his arms. The fog grew thicker, and above his head there was a big berblack gemonst all fuzzing and squeezie and down down down and squeezie fainted.

18

WHEN HE AWOKE THE SITE WAS BOMBED. THE STARS, even the moon, shone brightly on the rubble. The tins and old whistles, the dockets and packets and lids, the labels and old food, the dead messages and the slag were all covered in a soft coat of furry snow and the tracing of the wind on its surface gave it an impression of great depth. A cruel frost was penetrating his clothes, a cold wind was blowing round his legs, and he huddled inside his coat like a doormouse inside a winter. His head ached, but his brain was music-clear. Above his neck lay arctic wastes, and across his forehead jagged blocks of pack-ice slowly floated.

His first thought was that this was the top of the world. He looked around. Not a soul in sight. He stood up, and immediately felt ill. He leant unsteadily against a wall, and on an old tin, sheltered from the snow by a ruined corner-stone, there was a brief intermezzo in E-flat, and then silence. A rat stirred uneasily against its mate, and a touch of dawn appeared in the eastern sky. He began to see where he was. He was above the city, on the top of one of the hills, and far below him the spires of the churches were becoming visible in the increasing light.

Where had he been? He had difficulty in remembering. Drinking, of that he was sure. He recalled awakening in a strange room, fully clothed upon a bed, and feeling cold and ill. He remembered wondering where he was, and creeping stealthily out, in case it was somewhere unpleasant.

Every time he moved impressions ran through his head like butterflies impaled on pins in the pages of an album. He saw a woman, a comfortable woman. He saw a girl, a young girl seated in a train. The woman piled more fuel on the range, and the girl stirred in her sleep. Then both scenes faded before a wave of nausea, and he clung to something, anything, it was an old railing, where a garden had once been. The wind caught him, his coat swirled around his shoulders, and his body seemed to be stampeding past him in panic. He was sick.

He began to walk. The pain of cleaving the cold air soothed his nausea. He could see that the hill on which he was walking took the form of a ridge, and in front of him all signs of ruined buildings ceased and there was only barren earth, where perhaps there had been open-cast mining.

He stumbled into the submerged path that ran round the outside of an air-raid shelter. He sat against the wall where he had fallen and let his head fall back until he felt the pressure of the wall upon it. For a moment he slept, but then the light awoke him.

He groped his way into the hut, out of the reach of the wind, and gazed out at the growing dawn. It was angry, and patches of fierce cloud were approaching swiftly from the west. He recalled that other dawn which had been so very much less angry, and which he would have remembered more than a year ago, if Mrs Pollard had not disturbed him. He recalled the awakening of Miss Daisy Wilkinson.

He had awoken first. There had been steam on the windows, and the light had been very faint. She was sitting opposite him again, with her back to the engine. Grey slivers of dawn were beginning to rise, illuminating a huge carpet of snow which glowed light pink to the east and was sullen and purple elsewhere. The snow had stopped for some while and the winds had blown it off the line and piled it against the hedges.

92

Miss Wilkinson seemed to grow lovelier with every moment that she slept. Each clouded breath thumped his heart. His hands fluttered as if they wanted to take hold of her, but he turned back to the window and continued to watch the dawn. It was all pink now, and as he watched the pink deepened to a livid red, prior to bursting, and behind it, among the faint clouds, a series of suns arose, pale echoes spreading over the sky and tapering away into space.

The wheels began to beat their insistent promise more slowly. The dawn was over. The sky had burst. The sun rose steadily above the horizon. The sky took up its position behind it, and in the west, where the sky was still the colour of brawn, the last remnants of the night were steadily chased away. The injured monster stirred in its bandage of snow and began to sparkle.

Miss Daisy Wilkinson moaned, lifted her head as if to moo, and then flopped back into her seat again. The train slowed down still more. They were passing a wood, a plantation of young larches. The wood was left behind. A field. A road. On the road a green single-decker bus travelled slowly over the soft, grey snow. High in the sky a flock of rooks idled. The workmen in the bus wiped the windows with their hands and stared up at the wheeling birds. The travellers in the train rubbed their eyes with their hands and stared up at the wheeling birds. The scarecrows in the fields swung tinnily on their axes and stared up at the wheeling birds. The train slowed to a halt.

Miss Wilkinson blinked, sat up abruptly, and tossed back her hair reproachfully, as if it alone had been responsible for her sleep.

"Where are we?" she asked.

Lewis glanced at his watch.

"Ten past seven," he said.

She giggled sleepily. "You are a one," she said. "Never a dull moment with you around."

For a few dull moments there was silence. Then suddenly he understood her question and he said: "I don't know."

"What?"

"Where we are."

93

"Oh."

"We must be very late. We were held up for hours in the hills."

"I must have been asleep."

The train began to move once more. She stood up and attempted to comb her hair in the north transept of Hereford Cathedral. Her skirts rose above her knees, and he looked at the dimpled crack at the back of them. She sat down beside him when she had finished, and patted his hand. He could smell the sleep of her.

"Oh, Lewis," she said.

The pink in his face deepened to livid red, prior to bursting. Another day was beginning. She looked up at him expectantly and when nothing came she said: "It's been a very nice ride."

"I'm glad." He smiled at her.

"I had a good sleep."

He could think of nothing further to say. He was glad, absurdly glad, that she had had a good sleep, but no good could come of repeatedly saying it. She seemed disappointed that he said nothing more, but he could do nothing about that. He did not trust his impressions of her. At times he felt that she was fascinated by him, and he kept silent out of embarrassment on that account. Then he would convince himself that she had no interest in him whatever, and was holding his hand out of pity, and he would keep silent out of embarrassment on that account. He knew enough of girls to realise that in any case she would expect some reaction out of him, and he could think of none. Why it should be his duty to break the silence he didn't know, but it was. He had been born into a society in which it was so, and he must learn to bear it. He did his best, delving around frantically for a word, any word. All that came to him was the clackety-clack of the train. Of course he could say that. He could say: "It's funny, but I can think of nothing except the clackety-clack of the train." He could, but he didn't, and perhaps it was just as well.

Nothing came. Not a spark. No ignition. Her hand fell limply from his, and he hardly noticed. And then, suddenly, he wanted to be with her and was frightened that she would go. The train

94

was moving, it was impossible for her to get away, but it was no comfort to him. He turned to her to plead with her, and then he paused in panic.

"Rooks," he said.

"You are odd," she said, smiling, and then she added; "I love nature."

"Yes."

"There's not a lot in Bromley."

"I suppose not."

"Very little indeed. I'd like to move. See the world. Wouldn't you like to go on a tour, Lewis?"

"Yes."

"I suppose you're on one, in a way."

"A mystery tour."

They were talking!

"I suppose it's more business than pleasure with you."

"It won't be. I mean . . ." he paused.

"I know what you mean." He was glad she did, since he didn't. "And it's beautiful. No-one in Bromley would ever mean a thing like that."

Surely under the circumstances . . . but did he want to? There was so much that he had to achieve.

"I think we're reaching a town," said Daisy.

Sure enough, suburbs and railway yards were appearing on either side, and the train was slowing down. In a few moments they were sidling into a station.

"Crewe," said Lewis.

"But that's nowhere near London," said Daisy. "I'm on the wrong train. I'll never get home."

They removed their suitcases from the rack and stared helplessly at each other, each wishing that it was possible to burst into laughter and collapse into each other's arms. There was a great deal of bustle in the corridors as the train bumped to a halt, and as they waited their turn to face the cold winds on the platform he could feel her breath tickling his neck.

Once on the platform the crowd forced them towards the exits.

95

There, on the indicator board, they saw that there was a train to London in twenty minutes, but neither of them commented on that. Instead, Lewis said: "There's a train to Congleton in ten minutes."

"Congleton?"

"That's where I'm going."

"You said you didn't know where you were going."

"I didn't. But I do now."

"But why Congleton?"

"Why not?"

"Why?"

"I must go somewhere."

"What will you do there?"

"I don't know yet."

There was silence for a few moments. He was about to offer her his hand, not daring to offer anything further.

"Why not London?"

"Well, I – I can't explain. The train'll be off in a moment. I must go. Good-bye, Daisy." He held out his hand awkwardly, blushing.

"I'll see you off."

She followed him to Platform Three, and stood on the platform while he stood at the open window of his compartment. She wanted to jump on board the train with him, but didn't dare be so forward.

"You don't know how awful my life is in Bromley."

"I'm sorry. I can't help that."

"I don't know what I'll do without you."

"I – you've only known me for a few hours."

She looked embarrassed. He smiled weakly at her and she tried a watery smile in return, but it froze on her face.

There was a whistle and a hoot from the diesel.

"I think you're off," she said.

There was still time, and even when the train was beginning to move there would still be time. The sudden renewed uncertainty of it was dreadful, doubly so since they both knew what would happen. It would never be possible for Lewis to jump off. That sort of thing would never be possible.

"Don't miss your train," he said, choking lightly.

"What will you do?" she asked.

"I don't know. I'll find something."

The train began to move.

"Good-bye," he said.

"Good-bye."

"Look after yourself."

"Yes. Write to me."

"Yes."

"Promise?"

"All right."

But he never would. He hadn't her address. She was falling back now as the train gathered speed, but he felt compelled to wave and prolong the agony. He waved, she waved. He receded, she receded. He was just a speck, she was just a speck. It was over.

Now at last he could let the tears flow. He stood by the window, and they slid gently down his face. The train clanked rhythmically towards Congleton, and away from Miss Daisy Wilkinson, the great love of his life. For he knew now, as he sped away from her – and she from him – that he loved her, and that she loved him. He knew that through that wonderful and perfect love he would have found the purpose of existence with no trouble at all. It was too late now, but he knew that she was the only woman in the world for him, and as the distance between them increased at a hundred miles per hour his tears were accompanied by mild convulsions.

Having tied up the loose ends of his reverie and made himself even iller than before, Simpson felt the tears freezing on his cheeks and he remembered where he was. The dawn was almost complete now, and the wind was colder than ever in the last fierce spite before it gave way to the warmth of the day's activities. He clambered stiffly out of the submerged path and set off in the direction of Trebisall Avenue, sensing by instinct which road he should take. His steps were still unsteady and his head still ached, but now the full sun was shining brightly on him between the clouds. A new spirit entered his heart. He no longer doubted her, no longer wondered whether she would be awaiting him. This time – provided only that she was still alive – there would be no mistake. He felt a new sensation glowing within him, a feeling of being, or at any rate being about to be, Baker. From now on he would be a different man – bold, forthright, strong in word and deed. His new sense of purpose urged him on, and he walked swiftly through the steep, empty streets. This new sense swept joyously through his whole body, banishing his nausea as if it had never been, and he would have sung, had he not been tone deaf.

He reached Pantons. There, across the road, was Trebisall Avenue. Up there lay number 38. And somewhere in number 38, he hoped, was Mrs Pollard.

He knocked on the door. There was the sound of footsteps and heavy breathing. A face flattened itself against the frosted glass, and the door was slowly opened. Mrs Pollard stood before him.

"My love," she gasped.

19

BAKER SPENT THE NEXT FEW DAYS PRETENDING TO write poetry, and Mrs Pollard spent them pretending to find new recipes for her stews. Between them there had sprung up a deep restraint from the moment of her confession on the doorstep. The unexpectedness of it had prevented either of them from preparing any defence against it or any way of admitting it without awkwardness, and there were long periods when they had no conversation at all. From time to time Mrs Pollard made polite enquiries about his life in prison – she told him that she had read about the case in the *Telegraph and Chronicle* and had been embarrassed to come and see him now that she knew he had a wife – but they spoke impersonally. So great was the distance between them when they spoke that Baker was unable to summon up any misery at the memory that she had not come to see him in prison, whatever the reason.

Each day, when he was alone, he decided that, come what might, he would face up to the situation before nightfall. And each day, as darkness fell, he decided that it was too late and that it was better to wait until the next day, when she might be in a better mood and he might be feeling bolder. And the longer he did not broach what was in his mind, the harder it became for him to do so.

Mrs Pollard was experiencing the same difficulty with the added complication that, being his landlady, she didn't want to give the impression that she was being at all forward. She spent much of the time in Veal's room, but found that she did not get as much sympathy as she wanted. If anything was impervious in these troubled times, it was Veal. In fact she was finding more and more as the days went by that her visits to Veal were not having their old effect. Something had died. She still went to his room, to tend him and make him comfortable in a thousand little ways, but she went as a landlady rather than as a woman.

And so they lived under the same roof, in conditions that were rapidly becoming intolerable. And in the end Baker spoke. He spoke very calmly and quietly, as if he was no party to the utterance, and indeed he felt that he was not.

"I was wondering if it was a good idea if I came and took my meals with you," he said. "I'm getting rather tired of this room."

"I have no objection," said Mrs Pollard. "Nobody can ever say I didn't ask you." Their voices were quiet and muffled, as though a window had been closed between them.

And so, three times a day, Baker visited Mrs Pollard in her kitchen, and she poured rich stews from the casserole into great bowls, and they sat at either side of the huge black shining range, eating slowly and with satisfaction while great logs were burning on the fire and tracing mellow flashes on the thick stone walls.

"It's much nicer here than in my room," he said, and then he looked confused. "Not that my room is in any way inadequate for what I'm paying, but here . . ." his voice trailed away. He had been using the room for nearly a fortnight, but there was particular tension in the air that evening.

"You wouldn't think I was fifty one, would you?" asked Mrs Pollard.

"No."

"I've always believed in keeping myself fit. Not that I was ever what you'd call a natural athlete, but I've always kept fit. You never know. Take the bandages with you and somebody may bleed. And of course mother was a Methodist and it's not often you find Methodists running to seed."

As she spoke Baker was continually smiling and ceasing to smile, nodding and ceasing to nod, murmuring agreement and ceasing to murmur agreement. It was the sort of outburst for which nature had fitted her, and it was amazing that she had not launched on it before and that it was so short when it finally came. Baker found it restful to sit and listen.

"Not that I'm a religious woman," she was saying. "I'm not. There's no reason why, but I'm not. It's just that it's never really occurred to me to be, I suppose. I have my connections with the other side, I won't pretend I haven't, but it's not religious. It's just that I like to keep in touch. I've kept my end up, and that's more than can be said for some. Nobody's ever told me what to do. Not that I'm a sinner. Let's have that understood. I don't hold with it. It's like grumbling. You're happier without it. I've had enough to grumble about, but what's the use of it? Life's been hard to me. I've lost Pollard. I've lost them all sooner or later. It hurt, I don't mind telling you, but I got over it. Not that I don't miss them. They meant something to me. Things went on, I won't pretend they didn't. We had our moments, and what's the harm of it, when you're fond of someone? Don't wait for the crumbs and you won't go hungry. After all, what use are you if you're hungry? Fainting away all over the place, what good's that? It worries me sometimes, what Pollard would say. But then you see he had his consolation. But I mean, how can you just sit there, day after day, having your consolation, while all those poor Syrians are having another earthquake? Pollard couldn't see it that way. He was very good in the garden, green fingered, but a lot of things escaped him. Not that I'd run him down. Don't blacken the dead, and the dead won't blacken you. But you have to ask yourself, where's it all got him? He's been dead for nineteen years and I'm still as large as life. You can't get away from that."

Baker had no wish to get away from it, but he could see that if one did want to it might be very difficult. All he wanted to do was to love this woman. Not yet, though. The time was not yet ripe. First he must prepare the ground. So he spoke to her about his hopes, and told her how important it was all to be. He even hinted at what an important part she might have to play. For a woman who liked to do the talking herself Mrs Pollard was amazingly attentive. She was pleased to see him so talkative at last and flattered by his confidences.

"You've made me very happy," she said when he had finished. "I won't pretend you haven't. None of the others ever spoke to me like that."

"Tell me about the others."

"There was Pollard, of course, and poor Mr Veal. There still is him. And then there was poor Mr Grant. He died. And then there was Mr McGregor. He died too. Very quiet they were, Mr Grant and Mr McGregor, and shrewd investors both. Two eggs from the same hen. And then there was Mr Phelp. Quite a change, after the others. Always up to something, was Mr Phelp, and no table manners at all. He travelled in novelties. Many's the time I used to find mechanical lizards in my bed, but you couldn't hold it against him. He died, too. And then there was Mr Jennings. He was a footballer. He played centre-forward for the United, not that I've ever watched football. But I'll say this, I never had cause to complain about Mr Jennings. Sometimes he could be quite select, when the mood took him. I was very sorry to lose him."

"He died?"

"Mr Jennings die? Never. No, I transferred him to Mrs Bowen – 33, Cemetery Lane – for £3,000. I needed the money. It's my nest egg."

What could Mr Jennings have been like? Mr Jennings and Mr Grant and Mr McGregor and Mr Phelp and Veal? Veal especially. There were times when the thought of that silent presence preyed on his mind.

Sensing his feelings, Mrs Pollard said awkwardly: "And now I have you." She got to her feet.

"Sit down," said Baker imperiously, much to his amazement, and Mrs Pollard, who had never heard him speak in that tone before, could not have sat down faster if she had been the Archbishop of Canterbury.

The stern command of his gesture made it doubly difficult for Baker to follow it up, and there were several moments of confusion before he said: "What did you get up for?"

"To make some tea."

"We don't want any tea." He was upset by the failure of his gesture.

"Mr Jennings always had a cup of tea about this time."

"I don't want to hear any more about your Mr Jennings." He stood up, a thing he never did in company, unless it was to offer his seat to a lady. "It's been Mr Jennings this, Mr Jennings that all the time lately. If you're coming in on this thing with me we'll have enough on our hands without Mr Jennings."

He sank back into his seat, but the tension in the room had been increased as a result of this utterly inaccurate outburst, and the longer they sat in silence the greater it grew.

Eventually, when it was still a little before bed-time, Mrs Pollard stood up – a brave action, under the circumstances. Nor did she let things rest there. She stood with her back to the range gazing down at Baker, as if she had just come in after a hard day with the guns and he was a hearth-rug she had killed in Nepal. He felt sickeningly hollow.

"Before we go to bed," she said, "would you like to have a look at Mr Veal?"

He was astounded. Why now, after all this time? The way in which she had spoken suggested that he was being admitted to some inner sanctum and asked to share something that had previously been hers alone. He didn't like the idea of that, but on the other hand he did want to see Veal.

"I – yes, I – I don't want to intrude."

"I don't think you could intrude, not where Mr Veal's concerned."

"I've been wanting to meet him."

Mrs Pollard led the way up the narrow, creaking stairs. It was very dark. She was panting and having great difficulty in breathing, and before they went into Veal's room she waited for it to die down. "I always wait for it to die down," she said. "It's like taking your shoes off if you're Japanese."

Then she opened the door, and they entered the room. It was very small. Veal lay in bed from head to foot, entirely motionless. All that were visible above the blankets were his face and the head that surrounded it, and had once given it what depth it had. But it had no depth now. Veal was a skeleton now.

Mrs Pollard watched Baker's face anxiously, as if he was the art master and Veal was one of her paintings. He stood with his lips parted, gazing at the whitened bones on the pillow.

"Of course, you're not seeing him at his best. You should have come when he was younger."

Baker did not move.

"He's lost a lot of colour."

Baker did not show that he had heard.

"I wish I could get him to take something."

Baker did not show that he had moved.

"You can see how handsome he was."

In a low, cathedral voice Baker said: "And you loved him very much?"

"When he was younger."

"And you love him still?"

103

"No." Mrs Pollard slipped her hand lightly into his, and there was nothing he could do about it except shiver. "No."

"What did your husband think?"

"Pollard?"

"Yes."

"He never knew."

"Never knew?" Baker's eyes turned from Veal for the first time, and he glanced at Mrs Pollard.

"Nobody knew. Mr Veal least of all."

"But didn't he love you?"

"You've never really known him, have you?"

Baker took a quick glance at Veal before he said: "No."

"He's never exactly overflowed with love. Or hate. He's never been a man for overflowing. But now, lately, he's seemed to have less love than ever. And hate. Poor lamb."

Baker continued to stare intently at Veal. He wanted to look away, but he felt drawn towards the bed. He walked slowly forward, with his eyes fixed on the old man's face. He felt that he would bend down and kiss him. Just as, sometimes, in a train that was travelling particularly fast, his hand had been poised on the door of the compartment, and he had been on the point of opening it and jumping out for no reason at all, so now his face was poised over Veal's, and his body felt a thrill of horror that surged right through him. Then, just as in the train his hand would always fall limp, so the tension drained from his face and he wanted only to be sick. He went to the window, opened it with difficulty, and leant out. The cold air was refreshing, and soon he felt all right again.

"I'm sorry," he said, closing the window behind him. "I felt funny."

"It's with climbing the stairs," said Mrs Pollard. "You're not used to it. You ought to sit down." Baker sat down on a wooden chair which stood near the window.

"I've bad news for you," he said.

"Bad news?" Did she half suspect it already, he wondered.

"It's Veal. He's dead."

"Dead?"

"I'm afraid so." He led her gently over to the bed and pulled back the blankets. He laid her hand lightly where his heart had been. "There's no life in him." He was shivering.

"So he's dead," said Mrs Pollard, sinking into the hard chair. Baker rearranged the bedclothes as carefully as he could.

After the first blank moments Mrs Pollard began to feel a sense of loss, vague and unrealised as yet. "He was a good man," she said. "A good man."

Baker stood over her and patted her hand.

"So he's dead," she said again, as if to herself. "We must arrange the bed. Do it for me."

"How?"

"Just neatly. That's all. Well, well, it's been a long life. He's been a good lodger to me. That's right. Nice and neat."

Baker finished making the bed with great care, but, hard though he tried, there were creases and ruffles in it.

"I'll straighten it," said Mrs Pollard. "I've tended him long enough." With a few deft touches she smoothed the sheets and tidied the edge of the blankets. "Now we must cover him. There's a quilt in the next room."

Baker fetched the quilt and they laid it over the stiff body of the dead man. Then they lifted it back so that the head was revealed to them for the last time.

"He's sinking fast," said Mrs Pollard. She covered his face up again and they walked to the door. They paused before leaving the room to have a last look at the body where it lay under the quilt, and then they closed the door very swiftly with an immense feeling of relief, and tip-toed rapidly down the stairs. They sat for a few moments by the hearth, with the dying embers lighting their pale faces in the darkness of the room.

"We must get a doctor to certify death," said Baker.

"No."

"But he's dead."

Dead, yes, he was dead, but why certify it? Give him a chance, and you never knew. He might come back to life.

"Well, if we have to, fetch Dr Holdsworth."

Baker fetched Dr Holdsworth from his house in the next street. He soon finished his examination and met them in the hall with a long face.

"He's dead all right," he said. "It's not easy to estimate how long. Quite a long while, though. About June, 1948, I should think. I'll issue a certificate."

"Must you?"

"I'm afraid so."

Dr Holdsworth left them, and after a few moments Mrs Pollard asked: "Would you like a little something?"

"Ought we to?"

"I think he'd like us to." She shivered. "I suppose we must be missing him. You never miss people until they're gone, and then it's too late. I think we ought to have something."

"All right then."

"What will you have?"

"What is there?"

"Bovril."

"I'll have that."

Mrs Pollard made the bovril, and while the water was boiling and while they were drinking it she told him about Veal. She told him how it was in 1936 that he had appeared on her doorstep, impeccably moustachioed, in response to her advertisement.

Anxious to improve her furniture, she had persuaded Pollard to take in someone as a paying guest. Pollard had been forced to agree and Veal had been regarded as eminently suitable. He was so quiet. Of his past they had never known anything, and there were moments when he hardly seemed to have a future. It was his present that had endeared him to Mrs Pollard and made him grudgingly acceptable to her husband.

Veal had been a good tenant. For long periods he had just sat at home, working things out, as he called it. At first these spells of intense reflection had been interspersed with periods of violent activity. He would announce, one morning: "No bacon, egg or kidney, thank you. Just the juice of a fruit and a modicum of

106

lightly-browned toast. I'm in strict training." Then, after break-fast, she would hear him limbering up. Pieces of masonry would fall around her ears as he did his bicycle exercises, and sometimes the whole street would be a chaos of falling stones as he ran, discus in hand, round and round the imperfect triangle formed by Trebisall Avenue, Corporation Street and Bolsover Road. It had been an awful job, patching up the damage and concealing it from Pollard when he returned from work, but somehow she had managed it, and then Pollard had gone to war, and had not come back. But by that time the training sessions had become less and less frequent, the exercises less and less severe, until eventu-ally he took nothing more strenuous than a short walk every three months, then every six months, then never.

It was seventeen years ago, now, the June day on which he had last taken the air. The sky was blue, with an insistent threat of cricket, and already, at nine o'clock, it was hot. Suddenly Veal had set out on his last and shortest walk. Mrs Pollard had watched spellbound from the kitchen window. Every five minutes a leg was slowly raised, slowly urged forward, slowly lowered. He had not even reached the garden gate. Exhausted, he described a wide circle – to turn sharply was no longer within his capacity – which took him through the pitiful remains of what had once been, in Pollard's day, a bed of prize lupins and loganberry bushes. All the time he was staring up at the sky and as he returned to the house Mrs Pollard noticed that his brow was tight with concen-tration and furrowed with effort. Finally, after six and three quarter trying hours and eighty-one steps, he arrived back at the front door, having completed a walk of nine feet two inches straight in each direction, plus a circle of which the diameter was six. Once inside the house he seemed to have no difficulty in climbing the stairs and when she went up to his room to enquire about his bodily needs he had been in bed, in his pyjamas. He had remained there ever since.

At first there was a stream of callers, but after a few months it dwindled into a mere trickle of occasional visits from his brother and two friends from his flying days, R.A.F. Swabfleet and

R.A.F. Pangoose. Then his brother had stopped coming, then R.A.F. Pangoose, and then, finally, R.A.F. Swabfleet. No more rent was forthcoming. For Mrs Pollard it had become a labour of love.

"I hope you enjoyed the bovril," she said.

"Yes, thank you."

"We'll have the funeral next Tuesday."

Earlier. Please, he thought, please get him out of here earlier.

"Yes."

"I hope they'll all be able to come. His brother and friends."

"Yes."

"Ready?"

"I – yes."

"We'll leave the washing up. There's no-one to see. We're all alone in the house."

"He's still here."

"In a sense. Are you coming?"

"Tonight?"

"You aren't going to leave me alone, after that?"

No, he thought, I can't leave her alone, after that. And he didn't want to be alone himself, shivering and afraid, after that. And yet, not this. Not yet. Not tonight. Tomorrow, perhaps, but not tonight. He couldn't leave the shade of his own shadow now. The time was not yet ripe. Tomorrow . . . tomorrow . . . tomorrow . . . but Mrs Pollard was gazing at him, and waiting for him, and the will that impelled him was no longer his own.

20

WHAT COULD HAVE GONE WRONG? THEY HAD MADE love, and yet he felt no joy. He lay back with his head on the hard bolster, watching the leaves of morning sunlight kissing the chalky old ceiling, and yet he felt no joy.

It had not been as embarrassing as he had imagined during rehearsals. Mrs Pollard's age, his age, the darkness, the days and weeks that had led up to it, all these had helped to make it easier. It had happened, and under the circumstances it was deeply to be regretted that he had not experienced through his whole body sensations of joy and well-being so complete that he had woken up without even being aware that he had fallen asleep.

And then he remembered that a happy union is a thing that can come only slowly to fruition. Many people ignorantly believe that it will be roses and cream all the way. They are entirely unaware of the little strains and stresses, the problems of emotional and bodily adjustment, the personal difficulties and worries, the irrational fears, deep-seated prejudices, unhealthy complexes and crippling neuroses that will have to be overcome before they can experience that entirely new level of joy, creation, giving and understanding which can hardly even be imagined by those who have never experienced full union. It was not something that should be entered upon without a great deal of care, checking on one's hereditary diseases, balancing one's diet, and choosing for one's bedroom a wallpaper that would serve to alleviate the fears and sudden shynesses that spring up naturally in the early months of an intimate relationship. It would be difficult. It was bound to be. What was not difficult was not worth attaining. A heedless action might cause deep revulsion, which might take many months to overcome. A thoughtless word, practically *de rigueur* in the changing room at Twickenham, could cause a sensitive bride great pain. If they had only received an adequate sex instruction, and had not gone through life in such ignorance, it would be easier. Mrs Pollard, it was true, had a previous history of sex experience, but Baker was not so naïve as to imagine that in twentieth-century England those who were married, and even those who had produced perfectly satisfactory children, had necessarily experienced to the full the entirely new level of joy, creation, giving and understanding which can hardly even be imagined by those who have never experienced full union. Love comes only with perfect understanding, perfect sympathy, and in time they would attain to love. If, after several years, one party was still not taking part in the unions, they should see a doctor. Doctors are experienced in dealing with such matters. For the moment, however, they must be patient. They must not regard each other as faultless. There would be disagreements. Wouldn't life be rather dreary if people agreed about everything? No marriage is really healthy without its little tiffs, rows, quarrels, fights, separations and divorces. These things do not mean that it is a failure. On the contrary, they have an essential part to play in its eventual success. If they bore all this in mind, and remembered each other's anniversaries, and showed their consideration in a thousand little ways, they would come to know each other more intimately, sympathise with each other more perfectly, harmonise more completely, love each other more deeply, and attain to the universal panacea for all mankind more easily.

He smiled. Beside him Mrs Pollard slept, not yet the deep sleep of she who has been truly satisfied spiritually, physically and emotionally, but the sound sleep of one who is dog-tired. He smiled again. And even as he smiled he remembered. Veal was dead.

They were on the verge of great discoveries. For the moment, however, these would have to be postponed. There were the arrangements for the funeral to be made.

21

LOCAL AIRMAN - ATHLETE MOURNED

"No ordinary pilot" - VICAR

Friends from the worlds of aeroplanes and athletics this week mourned the death at his Trebisall Avenue home of the former test pilot and hurdler, Mr Philip Veal.

Born in 1899, the son of a prosperous Crewkerne butcher, Philip Veal was educated at Wellington and Oxford. His association with this area began when he was posted to R.A.F. Droppingwell in 1925. In 1929 he left the R.A.F. to become a civilian test pilot, and in 1936 he retired and went to live in Trebisall Avenue. He was unmarried and left no children. He had not been well since 1899.

Veal, who was elected Mr Ejector Seat in 1927, made his most vital contribution to aeronautical thought, ironically enough, in testing the ill-fated Harper-Doldrum Fretwork Amphiballoon, a portion of which can still be seen in Lowestoft Museum.

OSCAR

Second only to his achievements in the air were Veal's performances on the running track. Local enthusiasts will recall that he hurdled his way to victory in the Barnsley Invitation Handicap in 1933, when he was already a veteran of 34. He won the A.A.A. Championships 100 yards five times and added the 220 yards title on two occasions. He also won many victories on the continent of Europe.

His greatest recognition came in 1928 when he was awarded the "Athlete's Foot", a bronze replica of a foot presented each year by the Belgian Sports Writers' Association to outstanding European athletes.

CLEANER

Among the many dead present at his funeral service held in St Paul's Church, Purdle Dip Bottom, on Tuesday were: Mr Terence Veal, brother; Mrs Madge Pollard, landlady; Messrs R.A.F. Swabfleet and R.A.F. Pangoose, colleagues; Baker; Air Vice Marshal Sir Godwin Colander, Air Vice Marshal; Mr Tod "Biceps" Wallis, trainer and raconteur; Mr Eustace Begg, friend; Mrs Sally Turnover, cleaner; the Rev. E. A. Greensward, vicar; and Mr Alastair Bardwell, of the Amateur Athletic Association.

Paying tribute to the dead man, the Rev. Greensward spoke of his great death, but said that it would be a pity if this was allowed to overshadow his life. As he had lived that others might die, so had he died that others might live. Sacrifice, declared the vicar, has been a popular feature of all religions. What had the congregation ever sacrificed?

Veal had not permitted himself to die until he had lived. His sense of duty was too strong. The Rev. Greensward asked the congregation whether they had a sense of duty.

ALSO NEEDED

"There is still a great need for the right sort of men at the helm," he added. "We cannot live well-directed lives unless we have a pilot."

But a pilot needed not only an aeroplane. He also needed a landing-ground. And a landing-ground was a complicated thing. No aerodrome would be complete without its runways, hangars, luggage racks and restaurant facilities.

"In every gas heater there is a pilot light," said the Rev. Greensward. He told the mourners that Veal had by his example shed just as sure and constant a light on the world as that which burnt in their own Ascot heaters at home.

Ascot. The very word suggested gambling, snobbery, false pride. How far removed from such elevated and over-publicised gatherings were athletes like Veal, men who understood that life was a team game, that the spiritual must keep in training just as the athlete does, and that faith is the baton that we pass to our children in the relay race of life.

TRADITIONAL GLASS

The Rev. Greensward emphasised that Veal's death would be an example to his fellow men. There was no reason why, as a dead man, he should not scale heights even greater than those he had achieved during his lifetime. Some men devote their lives to the service of their fellows. Others, said the vicar, who spoke for seventy minutes, refreshing himself only once from the traditional glass of milk and honey, devote their deaths. Veal had devoted both. That was a measure of the man.

"Some people declare that the church as we know it today is antiquated and outmoded," he concluded. "It is, but some antiques are extremely valuable. They also cost a great deal to keep up. Only with your generous contributions can we continue to combat the death watch beetle."

22

THE COFFIN SLID NOISELESSLY INTO THE EARTH. A cold wind was blowing out of a clear blue sky, and they wore the collars of their coats turned up. They stamped on the ground with their feet, to keep their circulation going, Veal having made them aware of how important that is to the living. Their breath drifted south-westwards on the wind. What could they be thinking of, as Veal slid noiselessly towards the centre of the earth.

The Rev. E. A. Greensward was thinking about his funeral. It had been a very good funeral. They had been lucky with their weather. Soon, at the reception, they would feast, politely dissecting the corpse with knives and forks. Oh dear. But then that was life. None of your friends turn up when you're born but they're all there when you die.

Mrs Pollard was thinking of Veal. Handsome he'd been, you couldn't deny. But reserved. He'd never been very sociable, especially during his later years, but it was hard to think that he was gone. There was Baker, of course, but that didn't matter to Veal. She shivered.

R.A.F. Pangoose and R.A.F. Swabfleet were thinking of another sky that had been blue. A tiny speck had looped and rolled in that sky, had twisted and turned. When he had stepped out of the plane his skin had been rough and blue, but his eyes had sparkled. All evening he had sat there, not hearing what was said, and his eyes had sparkled. They were to see those eyes grow dull.

Mr Tod "Biceps" Wallis was thinking of a young man in a track suit. He ran steadily, smoothly, like a well trained machine, in the vast emptiness of the stadium. He leapt over the hurdles as if he was weightless. It was as if his limbs moved steadily of their own accord, while his mind flew free and away, to loop and roll till the end of time itself. Nobody was watching, except Mr Tod "Biceps" Wallis, trainer and raconteur.

Mrs Sally Turnover was thinking about the funeral. No-one had told her there was to be a funeral. Never mind, though. It had been well worth staying for. Down on her knees she had been, scrubbing the misericords, when it had started up. There had been no chance of escape. It had been awful the way she kept sneezing throughout the sermon. It was the detergent in the water. Turnover would be waiting for his dinner, but she'd stay till the end now. You owed it to the dead.

Mr Eustace Begg was thinking of a young man at the side of a moorland stream. The dark, tufted moor, ruffled by the wind. An old stone bridge. A cottage. Ruined walls. A stunted tree. A blue sky. How often they had sat there together, not speaking much, content in each other's company, and in their fishing. But had Veal been content? Had he just been staring, staring far beyond the stream, towards things that he would never see, beneath that blue sky? He was dead now.

Mr Terence Veal was thinking of his ulcer. He couldn't get to as many funerals as he used to in the old days.

Air Vice Marshal Sir Godwin Colander was thinking of Mrs Air Vice Marshal Lady Dorothy Colander. She'd be missing their golf. That fellow Veal would have been handy with a niblick.

Mr Alastair Bardwell, of the Amateur Athletic Association, was thinking of death. Was it just a disease, of which the chief symptoms were decomposition and total immobility? A fit of depression struck Mr Alastair Bardwell, of the Amateur Athletic Association.

And Baker? He was thinking of Veal. Why had he died? Had he found what he was looking for? Had his last years been a burden to him? Why had his eyes grown dull? Had he been happy? These were the questions he wanted to put to that face he had almost bent down to kiss. He felt wretched and heavy, and sorry for Veal. And he felt sorry for himself as well. His burdens seemed very great in that cemetery and at the funeral meal that followed. Mrs Pollard was engaged in quiet conversation with

Mr Begg, who spoke of the Veal he had known and invited her to visit him at his home in Woodland Close. Others were speaking of the Veals they had known and finding other topics of common interest. Baker found no such solace. He waited for the dark night to swallow him up.

23

ALTHOUGH VEAL HAD BEEN BURIED THERE WERE still a great many people who had not, and two such were Baker and Mrs Pollard. They were too busy for such things. They were about to enter on a period of their lives which would make all that had gone before it seem like a living death. They were about to enter a state of existence that cannot even be imagined by those who have never given themselves physically, mentally and spiritually to another being.

On their return from the funeral they banished their misery by keeping so busy that they forgot about Veal altogether. They threw themselves into their affair like divorcees grabbing for the bottle. In those first days there was an intensity of activity that would have amazed them both had there been any time left over for amazement. Each night they made true love, and then slept soundly, and each day they worked. They were happy to share those activities which had hitherto been the prerogative of one party – or of the other. They made their stews together. First Mrs Pollard would drop an ingredient of her choice – an onion, perhaps, or a turnip – into the casserole while Baker stood with his back to her. Then she would close her eyes while he chose his ingredient – a turnip, it could be, or an onion. And it was the same with their poems. First he would contribute a line – "where green the ivy spreads her throttling hands", it could be – and then he would cover up his line with a book and she would add

115

a line of her choice – "Beneath the bower I met my Robespierre", perhaps. The stews were inedible and the poems unreadable gibberish, but they thoroughly enjoyed the stews and believed that the poems were masterpieces.

It was a simple and quiet life that they settled down to as the days passed by. There was no need to work while they had Mrs Pollard's "nest-egg" to live on, and Veal was quite forgotten. They did not pay a single visit to a night club, nor would they have done even if there had been one within fifty miles. They were happy together, happy in the knowledge that as they adjusted themselves to each other they would grow happier still.

Another occupation that helped to pass the days pleasantly during this exploratory period when they were getting to know each other better, was the writing of letters. They did not care about the outside world but this lack of concern did not have any meaning unless they recognised that the outside world was still there. Letters were the answer. Twice a week Baker wrote to Mrs Pollard, and twice a week she wrote to him. They would read the letters over breakfast, in silence first, and then aloud. "It's from you, dear," one of them would say. "You're having a lovely time, and it's doing you a world of good." And then they would read the whole letter out loud. They filled the letters with jokes, for both of them liked a rattling good laugh over their porridge, bacon and eggs, toast and marmalade, and tea.

They also wrote letters to other married couples, chosen at random from the list provided by P.E.N. Friends Ltd. It was delightful to write to Mr and Mrs Elliot, and Mr and Mrs Lucas, and to receive letters back from them. They all filled their letters with jokes, because they all liked a rattling good laugh over their porridge, bacon and eggs, toast and marmalade, and tea. Mrs Lucas, perhaps, took the biscuit. Her letters were a perfect scream. But Mr Elliott's were not far behind, and these two made up for the more ponderous efforts of Mr Lucas and Mrs Elliott.

Much of the time, however, after the bustling activity of the first few days had died down, they just talked. It was nice to sit in front of the great kitchen range and tell each other of their troubles, their fears and inadequacies.

One day Mrs Pollard told Baker of her diffidence about her ability to help him in his schemes. "It's different for you," she said.

"What is? And what from?"

"You were educated. How can I help you with your schemes?"

"But you are helping. All this, this is part of it all."

"You need more. All this panacea or whatever it is, you need education. What chance have I? My father kept a bicycle shop in Hornchurch. What could I possibly learn about ethics?"

"Ethics?"

"It's a closed book to me."

"I used to do quite a lot of bicycling, when I was at school."

"Don't change the subject. You did philosophy and everything. The only thing I ever was was netball captain."

"You were captain of netball?"

"What use is it now? I've forgotten it all."

"I was never captain of anything at school. I'm not the type. I haven't the character."

Then he talked to her consolingly about her strength of character, her ability to lead and inspire. He grew depressed.

"But you," she said. "You've had achievements."

"What?"

"Your poems. You're creative."

"They've never got me very far."

"You've set your sights high."

"I've achieved nothing."

"What if they're not published. They're beautiful. I think so anyway, and I'm the one to judge. What have I ever created?"

"What about your stews?"

"Stews!"

"All right. Sneer. But your stews have at least been eaten. My poems have never been read."

"I've read them."

Then he told her about the failure of his efforts in the gastro-

117

nomy world, culminating in an action for damages after a safety pin had been found in a Welsh Rarebit at the New Vista Café, Ventnor. But he had other strings to his bow, she told him. He'd been a journalist. So he told her how this string had snapped, how during his brief spell in Droitwich he had involved the paper in libel actions – all of them lost – brought by the Anti-Massage League, the Friends of Fibrositis and the British Brine Baths Benevolent Association. By the time he had finished describing the havoc that he had caused up and down the country, he was thoroughly and utterly depressed, while Mrs Pollard was the soul of bonhomie, comforting him and dwelling on his virtues. She told him how exciting his life had been, how experienced he was, how much he had travelled, how brave he had been, while she had been stuck here in the protection of her own little house, never venturing further than the market, never attempting to better herself or others, until she was in the depths of despair, and he was brimming over with hope and determination for the future. Then he told her what a wondeful thing it was to have a home, and to be able to provide food and shelter and comfort for those who needed them.

And so the days passed on a perpetual see-saw of emotion, as they experienced alternately the sensations of needing the other person and being needed in return. While it was a great relief to be able to know that one was about to comfort the other person by reminding them of one's failures, inadequacies and worries, it was very distressing to know that one was about to be comforted in return by them for these same things. In their talking together, and being together, and sleeping together, they were still finding a kind of pleasure, in the sense that they would certainly not have wished to be without each other, but it was beginning to dawn on Baker that they were no happier than they had been before. There were times when he was happier, it was true, but at those moments Mrs Pollard was more miserable, and there were times when she was happier, but at those moments he was more miserable. They had got into a series of ruts and ridges and the only time when neither of them was miserable was when they met for a few brief moments, the one climbing, the other descending, and even at that time, although they were no less happy than they had been, they were no more so. If they had been able to remain in that position for the rest of their lives, their mean happiness would have been, if not particularly exciting, at least tolerable, but since their happiness was dependent on the fact that they were going to grow happier still, far happier than they had ever been before, it was impossible for them to remain in that position for the rest of their lives, or even for the rest of the afternoon, once they realised the situation. Baker became quietly miserable, and he could see that Mrs Pollard, who, if the laws of the see-saw had still been operating, would have been in a state of tranquil ecstacy was very nearly as miserable as he. The honeymoon was over.

There were no recriminations. There was no expression, between them, of their knowledge that things had gone wrong. No voice was raised. Two adults had entered into a glass-house, smashed its panes with their clumsy elbows, and stepped out again. For a while life continued much as before, except that the joy had gone out of it. It was no longer pleasant to eat vile stews, so shortly Mrs Pollard resumed full responsibility for the cuisine, and it was no longer amusing to read bad poems, so Baker became sole executor of that side of the business. Even the letter writing came to an end after Mr Elliott, who liked his women to be a real scream, had run off with Mrs Lucas for a life of riotous wisecracks, leaving Mrs Elliott and Mr Lucas to cohabit in humourless gloom, without a pun to their names. Baker noted in his diary: "Constant Moping."

He made great efforts, during this time, to work out what had gone wrong and why the complete transformation that they had envisaged had not taken place. There were lots of possibilities – far too many for his peace of mind – and he had to deny himself even the satisfaction of knowing what his mistake had been, and promising himself not to make it again. He became convinced, in the course of his reflections, of one thing only – that it was all his fault. He was used to thinking this, and so it came easily to him.

He even began to finger imaginary coils of rope, and imagine himself in gas-filled rooms. What point was there in remaining alive, when life had treated him so harshly? "What have I to lose?" he thought to himself. "I've no relatives, no commitments, no promises, no godparents, no dependants, no furniture, no prospects, no achievements, no qualifications, no chums, no secret trysts, no debts, no engagements, no obligation. I'm virtually a liquid already." Why continue to live in a world which didn't want this wonderful gift he had to offer? They'd be sorry when he was dead. They'd gather round the newly dug grave, shivering with guilt.

But he did nothing, and intended nothing. He hung on, in an atmosphere of increasing claustrophobia, which would either throttle him or cause him to burst. He felt that he did not want to burst, for whatever it was that he shared with Mrs Pollard still remained, and he had no wish to lose her. It was a comfort to know that she was there, at the other side of the range, and that her thoughts were often turned to him, and that presently she would make bovril. But the walls closed in on him, the bronze pans leered disagreeably at him, and he felt that at any moment his nerves might snap and he might sink to the floor. Mrs Pollard kept looking through her photograph album, again and again and again, at faded grimaces on faded lawns.

Then he began to feel the stirring of blood in his veins. Little trickles gurgled here and there through his body, and he remembered how much he still had to do, and realised that if he had lived forty years without Mrs Pollard once he could do it twice, old age permitting. Quite soon now he would lurch out from his cage into a teeming world, all the fresher for his absence from it. To turn his back upon the great mass of humanity, and to expect to find the purpose of existence – their existence, as well as his – in a private and personal relationship was ridiculous. Whether he liked it or not – and he had absolutely no idea whether he did – he was one member, and Mrs Pollard was another, of a complex and highly-developed society. It was out there, in the midst of that society, that he must go. He would be ridiculed, of course.

He must put up with that. But there was no escaping it. It was out there that he must go.

He had been there before, it was true. Many times. But then how many great works of art would ever have been created if artists had always been discouraged by their early failures? Twelve. How many scientific discoveries, too, would ever have been made, and, once made, would ever have been believed, but for the perseverance of brave and devoted men? Three. Perhaps he would die in the attempt. Perhaps his triumph would come too late to benefit him. What matter? What matter if he died in poverty and obscurity, provided his work lived on? Future generations would know of him, future historians would write of him, future waxworks would exhibit him, as the man who discovered the universal panacea for all mankind, and gave it to all mankind.

Tomorrow he would go out there and start, after a good night's sleep. He leapt excitedly to his feet, and went to his room, forgetting that he now slept with Mrs Pollard. She followed him, anxiously, terrified, but he told her that he was tired, that he thought he was sickening for something, that he'd better sleep alone.

"You need comfort when you're sick. What am I here for? Didn't I console Mr Phelp when he had the blisters? What are women for?"

"It's not that. I'm not ill."

"Ill, not ill, I don't know. Make your mind up."

"I'm sorry. I've work to do."

"Work! You're suddenly busy."

"I've got to go out to work."

"At this time of night?"

"No. Tomorrow."

"Well then."

"I have to be alone tonight, that's all. It's like that sometimes."

"Is it?"

"Yes."

"I didn't know."

"I'm sorry."

She had gone, with dignity. For a few moments he contemplated her steps and wondered sadly what it would be like to be her at that moment. Then his blood swept him away and his nerves danced to his head. He grabbed hold of the sofa and converted it into a bed in a series of convulsive, screeching jerks.

Then he cleaned his teeth, undressed, placed his clothes untidily over the back of the wooden chair, tightened the cord of his pyjamas, and crept into bed.

Then he crept out of bed, switched off the light, and crept back in again.

24

HE WAS UP EARLY AND WAS SITTING IN HIS EASY CHAIR by the time Mrs Pollard came in with an enquiry about breakfast.

"Still loafing, I see," she said, having slept badly.

"I'm off to find a job after breakfast."

"I should think so, too. Loafing around the house in your bedroom slippers all day, and you a grown man."

"I don't have any bedroom slippers."

"You know perfectly well what I mean. I don't know. Versifying till all hours. It's not right. Will you have bacon and egg?"

"Thank you. I'll go down into the town and get a paper and see what jobs there are. Another lot of things I'm not suited to, I expect."

"Well, don't expect me to sympathise. Loafing around the house with your famous arrears of rent. There comes a time. Cereals or porridge?"

"Cereals, please."

"There comes a time. There's not many would have stood it as long as I have. No rent, and dried skin from your warts all over the house. Marmalade or honey?"

"Marmalade, please."

"Yes, well, there you are then."

Mrs Pollard went to make his breakfast and returned with it after a few minutes. She watched him in that manner that irritated him so much, but he forebore to mention it, and in a few moments she started up again.

"You come here, you take advantage of me with your panacea this, panacea that, you egg me on, you make me think your poems will bring us untold riches, you eat me out of house and home, you get me so that I don't know which of us is coming and which is going, you make me risk my reputation, without which no Darby and Joan club will look twice at me, and all for what? What's come of it, that's what I want to know. If Pollard was alive I'd get him to thrash you. Not that he would. He was a Pacifist. Until the war came, of course. After that, there was a war on, so of course he couldn't be a Pacifist. Pacifist or no, though, he'd see to you. He'd give you panacea. A fine universal whatever it is you've turned out to be, and no mistake. Though that's what you are, a mistake. That's just what you are. You're the biggest error of judgment that ever wiped its feet on my mat."

Suddenly Mrs Pollard was sorry, and could not say so. Baker knew it, and could not say so either. He thanked her for his breakfast and began to tidy himself up, and Mrs Pollard left his room with his tray, saying, with apparent irrelevance: "Don't say I didn't warn you."

He went out the back way, through the yard and down the alley, where a little boy was bouncing his sister against a wall. At the end of the alley he came to a little park, and behind the row of trees at the end of the park he could see the purple buses on routes 21 and 44 making their way to the city, and he could enjoy a delicious moment of anticipation. He wrung his hands together with a surge of excitement as he thought of all the activity of the world, of everything that he had missed in these last weeks.

He reached the streets and plunged into them, savouring, as he went, the diverse smells of city life, which contrasted sharply with the clean scent of the wind as it brought a promise of snow. He ventured far down hillside terraces that he had not visited before. He hacked his way through the warm stench of drying clothes and soapy mops. An occasional detour was necessary to avoid the fermenting brown air outside a pub, or the heat of cabbage pouring thickly from a toothless old window, but his progress was good. He placed his feet firmly, confidently, on virgin pavement which no Baker had ever trodden, and his passage through that strange place could have been charted from the cries that rose before him, as cats screeched away at the unfamiliar tread and noisy children ran to windows to peer and shriek. Eventually he heard a roaring ahead that grew louder and louder with each step that he took, and suddenly he found himself among the banks of a swiftly flowing city.

Ahead, on a hill, rose the principal buildings, and he climbed towards them. To his left were shops, offices and insurance companies, and over to the right the terraces of houses had once continued. But now a great scheme of slum clearance had begun. A huge crane was swinging slowly above the houses and on the end of its chain there was an iron punchbag, which swung against the walls of the modest houses soullessly and in slow motion. Clouds of red dust were rising into the air, and a few families, whose homes these had been, stood mesmerised into submission. All around offices and flats and schools of technology were rising, or stood as models on the desks of well-dressed men. Baker was badly dressed, despite his efforts.

On the cleared site, where as yet there had been no building, things sprawled, and a few people wandered among them. Here there was hard mud and clay and stone, bits of blue china, broken bricks embedded in frozen soil, and all manner of things that gave him quiet pleasure. On the centre of the site a bonfire was breathing on the air and turning it to shimmering frosted glass. Burnt scraps of paper climbed like rising snow, and a small group of people stood around the fire in silence, watching. For these few moments Baker's destination was quite forgotten. This glowing magnet claimed him. Flames flickered, shapes were created and destroyed, and people stared. There was something in the fire that thrilled all his senses and made him throw up his head into the cold air with pride.

He glanced at the men around him. They were looking into the fire not for what they might see but to blind themselves with its brightness. They were the few who were not busy at that moment in all the big buildings all around, and they were trying to blind themselves with its brightness.

He turned back to the fire. It was fine to succumb to the heat, to throw one's legs on the fire and then one's arms, and then one's brains. It was fine to stand by the fire and watch one's brain burn and one's thoughts turn to smoke around one's head. It was lovely to melt, and to feel the molten blood lapping round one's legs, rising, rising.

A puff of wind pushed the tangy smoke back into his face, and he coughed and turned away. His pride returned, and the fire burnt fiercely. At this moment, in Hertfordshire, they were dressing for polo. He'd show them. A new age was coming. There was so much to do, and at last he had the power. Onward. To battle. Sir Baker, rise.

Sir Baker strode mightily across the derelict site, and, forgetting that traffic had been invented since he set off to rescue his world in distress, stepped off the pavement straight into the path of a number 12 bus, which screamed to a halt a few inches from him. It gave him a terrible shock.

Baker continued to the top of the street, his heart thumping, and bought a copy of the *Telegraph and Chronicle*. Once again the "situations vacant" column consisted almost entirely of vacancies for those who already held jobs identical to those that were being advertised. The only feasible ones this time were for postal workers and, again, for bus conductors. It was obviously impossible for him to return to the buses, so he would have to try to become a postman.

He went straight to Postal Buildings and entered a door marked "Enquiries". He explained why he had come and a pretty girl gave him a booklet entitled "It's just the job!" and told him to sit down and wait while she rang Mr Lomax. He sat down, and while he waited he read all about the postman and his function in society. He was thrilled and inspired by all the services that he would have an opportunity of rendering, for it was through giving service, he realised now, that the purpose of existence was to be found.

"Mr Lomax will see you tomorrow," said the pretty girl, breaking in upon his prospects of bliss. "Eleven-thirty sharp. Through the swing doors in Haggle Lane, lift to the sixth storey, and it's room 13,002."

"Thank you."

It hurt him rather to think that they were no more eager to see him than that, when he had worked himself up into such a state on their behalf. And yet he was glad of the delay. While he was reading the booklet an idea had come to him. It was little more than a germ as yet, but he would work on it that night and it would swell into something far greater, something which in the weeks to come might revolutionise the General Post Office – and transform a nation's mail!

25

MR LOMAX WAS A GLOOMY, AGGRESSIVE LITTLE MAN who looked as though sealing wax wouldn't melt in his mouth. He motioned Baker into a chair.

"So you want to join the Post Office?"

"Yes, sir."

"I see. Ever done any postal work before?"

"No, sir."

"I see. Have you come straight from school?"

"No, sir."

"I see. What positions have you held, then?"

"I was a bus conductor, sir."

"What made you give that up? Eh?"

"I was sacked."

"Why?"

"It wasn't my vocation."

"And that's the only job you've ever had, is it?"

"No, sir. I've been a cook."

"A cook?"

"Yes, sir."

"I see. Anything else?"

"Yes, sir. A journalist. A schoolmaster. A seismographer. Several things."

"And what made you give all these jobs up? Eh?"

"I was sacked, sir."

"Why?"

"They weren't my vocation."

"Do you think this would be your vocation?"

"Yes, sir."

"I see. Why?"

"Because the Post Office offers a unique chance to help oneself and others at the same time, sir. There are posts for those who have just left school and want to lead an outdoor life, and for those who have graduated from the University and want to lead an indoor life. The Post Office offers stimulating horizons to those who are really keen. If there were no postal services, sir, this country would be subject to untold misery. No-one would know what anyone else was doing! To many people the postman is a symbol of hope. He it is who brings the good news that alters their whole life. He delivers letters alike to the big block of luxury flats in the heart of the thriving city and to the humble stone cottages in the midst of the lonely moor. His work cuts right through the invidious class distinctions that bedevil so much of our life today, sir. He brings the Christmas gifts while the snow is on the ground, and during the summer months he carries his heavy mail bag through the afternoon heat without wilting. He has a cheerful . . ."

127

"What makes you so sure we'd make you a postman if we employed you?"

"Well, sir, I – that was the vacancy in the paper, sir."

"Eh?"

"That was the vacancy, sir."

"Postal services, that was the vacancy. Ever seen an iceberg, Baker?"

"No, sir."

"No. I'm going to tell you something about icebergs, Baker. Icebergs have a little bit above the water. All the rest is underneath. You didn't know that, did you?"

"I knew that, sir."

"Nonsense. And what makes you think you'd be that little bit?"

"Well, I——"

"Where were you educated?"

"Cambridge and Winchester, sir."

Mr Lomax looked gloomier and more aggressive than ever. He leant forward and gazed fixedly at Baker. "There have to be backroom boys, you know. We can't all do the glamour jobs," he said.

"I want to be a postman, if I can. I want to deliver the mail."

"Why?"

"I've worked out a system, sir."

Mr Lomax stared at him even more fixedly than before, if such a thing were possible, before he said, very quietly: "Tell me about it, Baker."

"A – well, sir, it's a – a better method of delivering mail." The remark sounded meaningless when addressed to Mr Lomax, and Baker felt like a man in the first hot bath he has had for weeks, who has dislodged the plug with his foot and can't fix it in again in time.

"Better, Baker?"

"Well, sir, fairer. It seems to me that all the popular people, with lots of friends, get practically all the mail. The others, who need it most, get very little. Eighty per cent of the mail is going to twenty per cent of the population."

"And what do you intend to do about it?"

"Well, sir, I've worked out a points system." He took an untidily folded piece of paper out of his inside jacket pocket and handed it to Mr Lomax, who stared at it for a few moments.

"Explain."

"A Christmas card or a circular counts one point, postcards count two, letters three, registered letters and parcels four. Bills would be minus one. I would deliver ten points per head to every house in turn, and then if there wasn't enough mail to go round I'd remember where I'd stopped and I'd start there the next day."

26

DR MILDWEED'S MOBILE MENTAL HOME HAD BEEN pitched in a sheltered part of Roundwood Park, far from prying eyes. As one approached it, one could see, above the exotic trees of the botanical gardens, the huge tent where the cures were effected. One could catch an occasional glimpse, through the rare tropical shrubs, of the gaily painted caravans where the various specialists lived. They were a colourful people, those men and women of the road, men and women whose talents had been handed down from medical journal to medical journal, and sharpened by constant training. And one might also see, behind that gay scene, if one looked hard enough, the cages and wagons where the patients were housed.

There were not many dangerous patients at Dr Mildweed's. That was the great advantage it had over the Goldplank or City Mental. The Home remained for only two months in each city and dealt only with such patients as stood a good chance of being cured in that time, so there were none of the incorrigible lunatics who made life at the Goldplank so dismal and practically ensured that each new inmate was driven mad within a few days of his arrival, even if he had not been mad before.

This advantage would have seemed minimal to Baker, even if he had been aware of it. There could be no advantage to him in spending almost two months in a Home. He wasn't an old lag who liked an occasional spell of institution food at the small cost of having to pretend to believe that the Jehovah's Witnesses were out to get him. He wasn't even a family man, happy to abandon the monotony of his bungaloid life for a few weeks and enter a gayer and more inventive world. He was a man with a mission, a man with a vital function to perform, and now, when at last he had developed a framework within which to begin his task they had whisked him off to this horrid place. It was incomprehensible.

On their arrival at the Home a tall thin man with a black beard came to meet them. Fitted mentally and physically for only one thing, military dictatorship, Dr Mildweed had suffered the crippling blow of being born an utter coward in Worksop – a town little renowned for its *coups d'état*. So he had made the best of a bad job, had qualified in America as a doctor of some obscure corner of medical science, and had returned to England to set up Mental Home. Now he welcomed Mr Lomax warmly and ignored Baker completely. Mr Lomax was led off for a cocktail, while Baker was taken to Wagon Five, where, as a new inmate, he would be given a room to himself until diagnosis had been made.

In his little room he soon began to feel martyred. Here he was, in this dismal little cell, seven foot by five, and bare except for a bed, a chair and a bedside table with an empty fruit bowl on it. Here he was, at his time of life, in this situation which had come upon him too suddenly to seem real as yet, just when he could have cured the world. It was galling. But still, he was not the first man to be martyred, not the first man in the troubled course of our island's history – but at this point his thoughts were interrupted. A nurse wished to know – or pretended to want to know – the state of his bowels.

During the next half hour seven more nurses, due to an administrative mistake, questioned him on this same point. Long before the end his feelings of martyrdom had collapsed and his confinement had become a real situation. He began to be frightened, to wonder what they would do to him and where it would all end. He wished to question every nurse, to say: "It won't be too bad, will it?", to ask for little crumbs of comfort. But he dared not. He said: "No, I haven't been," and that was that. He wished he had never gone to the Post Office, and he longed to be back in Mrs Pollard's kitchen. He would have given a great deal, just then, to be back in Mrs Pollard's kitchen.

He was given a frugal supper for which he had no stomach. His growing fear held him in a clammy grip round the waist, and his throat was too dry for food. He knew that he was not mad, but he knew too that his knowing sprang from a knowledge of himself which nobody else could have. Without it they could call him mad, and probably would. There were always reasons enough.

He went to the window and tried to calm his fears. He looked up through that opening, barely more than a slit. Low clouds were scurrying above the rare shrubs and the tops of the giant firs were waving before a stormy wind. Between the clouds he could see an occasional star.

"I am Dr Mildweed," said a voice, and he froze in a constricting vice of fright. "Sit down."

Baker went to his chair and sat down.

"Stand up."

Baker stood up.

"Sit down."

Baker sat down.

"Stand up."

Baker stood up.

"Sit down."

Baker sat down.

"Stand up."

Baker stood up.

"Sit down."

Baker sat down.

"How many times would you go on doing that, before you disobeyed me?"

Baker was silent.

"I asked you a question."

"I don't know, sir."

"We might find out, one of these days. You're Baker, aren't you?"

"Yes, sir."

"You can be cured, Baker, but it's entirely up to me. Don't forget that, and you won't go far wrong. Some of the things we make you do may seem rather odd to you, but everything's in your best interests, so relax. We have a great tradition here. *Mens sana in corpore sano.* I believe you fellows can be cured and there are strings of sane men wandering around England to prove it. I've got hundreds of testimonials from people who are tasting sanity for the first time in their lives – and liking it. People who believed they were congenital misfits are pulling their weight in society just like anyone else. So there we are, Baker. We pay you the compliment of believing that we can cure you. If you've any decency left you'll do the same. Now tomorrow Dr Grainger and I will have a chat with you and see if we can't sort out what it is that's wrong, and when we've decided that, you'll be put in the hands of a specialist. You'll see quite a lot of him. We've one doctor to every six patients here. We're a kind of mental Millfield. I see you've refused your supper. Why?"

"I wasn't hungry, sir."

"I was ravenous this evening. Surely you could have been slightly hungry?"

"No, sir."

"We'll cure that death wish of yours. We'll make you hungry, don't you worry. Starvation rations. We'll put you on starvation rations, Baker," said Dr Mildweed, and he set off again on his post-brandial tour, taking the uneaten supper with him.

Left to himself, Baker began to develop a large stomach for which he had no supper. The very word 'starvation' was sufficient to make him hungry, for hunger was a thing of which he was terrified. There had always been people to nourish him. Mrs Bell, Mrs McManus of Newport (I.O.W.), Mrs Pollard, H.M. The Queen. Even in prison he had had food, but he sensed that here the rules no longer applied. They could do what they liked with him here.

Soon it was time for sleep, and he crawled into his narrow, squeaking, slightly damp bed. On either side of him other patients, separated from him by walls, were crawling into their narrow, squeaking, slightly damp beds. He lay wakeful, worrying about his hunger, afraid for his safety, stifled by the airless, centrally heated little room and the walls that seemed to slide in on him all night. Outside all was silent. Nothing stirred in the municipal park. Frightening fancies began to take hold of him. Perhaps there was nothing outside at all, nothing except a wide emptiness, as far as the pain could stretch. Or perhaps what seemed to be a room was the only open space that remained in the world, the busy, built-up world, and he was in the only bit of open air there was, outside a world of rooms. He tried to brush these fancies away as his sweat began to hang on the air. A pale red night-light was burning, shining through a grille above the door and casting a hellish glow, bathing the bare little room in the colour of weak medicine. Outside the room, in the little hall by the door of the wagon, a male nurse struggled with a paperback by the light of a shielded torch. Baker could hear the rustle of the pages, as his hunger bit acid holes into his lining and the wounded night throbbed slowly on. The male nurse made cocoa. A spoon banged sharply against a tin cup. Six bells, and still the engines throbbed. On and on they sailed, sliding slowly downhill to the left, floating irrevocably across Oceanus towards the edge, until suddenly he was fully awake again, just as they tottered on the rim of the pit of emptiness. He screamed. The male nurse rushed in, saw that nothing was wrong, explained that it had all been a dream, and returned to his paper-back. Baker lay wakeful, all fancies gone, aching with hunger. And at last the dawn began, turning the *vin rosé* of the night to an angry grey. The night was over.

Breakfast, to his great relief, was normal, but lunch, he was told, would see the beginning of his starvation diet. After breakfast he was kept waiting in his little room until eleven, and then he was escorted to Dr Mildweed's luxuriously appointed caravan. The doctor greeted him courteously, introduced him to Dr Grainger, and motioned him into the easiest chair in which he had ever sat. It would have been impossible for a chair to be any easier without becoming a complete walk-over. It grasped him softly and insidiously to its bosom, and its great springy cushions jerked him up and down as if he was a balloon being tossed on pockets of air.

"Well, and how are you feeling this morning, Baker?" inquired Dr Grainger with that unassertive affability that had endeared him to Free Foresters up and down the land.

"Hungry," said Baker.

Dr Grainger wrote in his notebook: "A desire for affection."

"Relax," barked Dr Mildweed, and Baker shuddered, accentuating the movement of the chair. "Have a cigarette."

"I don't smoke."

"Stuff and nonsense."

For a few minutes they chatted casually, those two doctors, yet all the time they were circling round him, waiting to pounce. Baker, immersed in clouds of cigarette smoke and coughing at the impact of the unfamiliar fumes, was acutely ill at ease. He was only too well aware that his bouncing upon the cushions had sent his socks scurrying to his ankles in search of seclusion, leaving two expanses of white leg bare to the elements. He wanted to hitch them up but dared not move for fear of setting the chair off again. It had settled now, and he felt, as he sank deeper and deeper into its folds, that it was sucking him up like an insect-eating plant. His nose was running, as it always did at interviews. An itch had developed in his left armpit – always the first to go under duress – but he dared not move. Dimly he could hear the two doctors talking away, trying to draw him out by discussing certain minor difficulties they experienced – giving up their seats to women under the age of thirty-eight, urinating under way on board ship, and so on – and hoping that he would tell them of similar difficulties that he experienced. Eventually they had to ask him, so silent did he remain, and he told them that he found everything difficult. "Yes, yes, yes, don't we all, but there must be something you find the most difficult of all," said Dr Mildweed, and Baker explained that the more difficult a thing was the more difficult he found it. The easy he found difficult and the difficult he found impossible. Dr Grainger explained that nothing was in itself more difficult than anything else. We just chose to find it so. Baker said that he didn't choose to find anything difficult. Dr Grainger explained that we chose to find things difficult, without realising that we were doing so, because we didn't want to do them. Baker said that he didn't want to do them because he found them difficult.

The two doctors abandoned this impasse and began once more to chat to Baker. He began once more to gather up as much resistance to them as he could muster. It was tempting to feel relieved at the prospect of human contact, to speak intimately to them and feel the tensions melt around his mouth, but he knew that once that happened he would end by describing his childhood. He would tell them all about his mothers, and they would sit there, turning over the rich earth with their beaks, growing fat on the worms and grubs.

Once again he forced them to ask questions, and these he refused to answer. He pretended to have a bad memory, until they told him that you only lock the cupboard door if there are skeletons inside. He said that he did not wish to talk about the past, and the moment that he had said it he realized that they would take it as an admission of guilt. So he decided to keep silent, to ignore entirely the relentless questions from which all pretence of casualness had now been dropped.

"You know you're not being very helpful, Baker," said Dr Mildweed at length.

"We must find out something about you if we're to help you," said Dr Grainger.

Baker remained silent.

"Your silence is more revealing than any words could be," said Dr Mildweed.

"Then I'll go on helping. I'll stay silent," said Baker.

"Aren't you pleased to be in my mental home?"

"No."

"We can cure you."

"There's nothing wrong with me."

"Then why are you here?"

"I don't know. You tell me. I was brought here, that's all I know. I don't know why. Why must you question me?"

There was a silence. Then, very quietly, very calmly, very reassuringly, Dr Grainger spoke.

"You don't know why you're here. We don't know why you're here. Don't you see how important it is that somebody should find out?" he said.

But Baker did not answer. He had been made to say more than he had intended, there could be no denying that. He had been put on the defensive, he felt nervous and very confused, and he had been forced to cry out. But from now on he would reveal nothing.

"You feel we're getting at you, don't you?" said Dr Mildweed.

Baker did not answer.

"You feel we're prying into your private life."

Baker said nothing.

"You're on the defensive, aren't you?"

Baker remained silent.

"Why are you on the defensive, Baker? What are you frightened of?"

Again there was no reply.

"Well, Grainger, he's all yours. Take him away."

There was an agonised moment in which Baker felt that the chair would not yield him easily. Then he was on his feet, being escorted by Dr Grainger to the Art Caravan, where he was introduced to Nurse Almond, a beautiful young brunette. Dr Grainger explained that he would see him every day from eleven to twelve, and that there would be a group session each day at four. The rest of the time he would be engaged in creative activities.

Nurse Almond gave him the basic utensils with a delightful smile and explained that he could paint a stone bust of Dr Mild-

136

weed, provided for the purpose, a vase of plastic daffodils, ditto, or the real snow that was filtering down outside the window. But he was not going to be caught as easily as that. He thought of the first colour that came into his head – it was green – and covered his canvas with a wishy-washy light blue.

For lunch he had a tiny rissole and three small pieces of potato, and afterwards he felt too hungry to paint. At four o'clock he had his first group therapy, but felt too hungry to concentrate. And then he waited in his room for a supper which was very similar to his lunch, except that the potatoes were slightly smaller. That night the acid emptiness that tore his stomach to shreds was far worse than on the previous night. A great weariness and weakness filled his head and legs, but he didn't sleep a wink.

In the morning he was so overcome by hunger that he was incapable of painting or of responding to questioning. He no longer had the energy to be miserable, and Dr Mildweed, making his morning rounds, realised that by pandering to his death wish they had made him very happy, and virtually dead. He must be brought back to life and all its problems. During the rest of the day, therefore, he was given no treatment. He was allowed to rest, and was brought back by gradual stages to a normal diet. And that night the order went out: "Patient No. 220. Vast feasts."

The next morning, after a breakfast of porridge, kedgeree, egg, bacon, sausage, kidney, tomatoes and fried bread, toast and marmalade and tea, Baker had a painting session, during which he produced two more light-blue canvasses. After his elevenses – three sticky buns and cocoa – he had another unprofitable talk with Dr Grainger. More painting followed, without issue, and then it was time for lunch.

Under strict supervision, he was forced to eat for his lunch Brown Windsor soup with roll, followed by enormous platefuls in swift succession of fried plaice, shepherd's pie and two veg, rissoles and two more veg, treacle tart, apple pie, jam sponge, and cheese and biscuits. During the afternoon he was given another painting session, in the course of which Dr Grainger returned to find out how he was getting on.

"Well, nurse, how's he getting on?" he asked.

"He's been sick all over the canvas."

"Good. He's beginning to express himself. Now that he's got that off his chest he should go on to something more subtle, some more positive way of expressing his self-disgust. This is where things become interesting. Don't stop him, nurse, whatever he paints. Even if . . ." and here he began to speak in that fatherly, protective tone which Nurse Almond found that older men used to brunettes, as if it was only by leading sheltered lives that they had avoided being dyed blonde. "Even if it's obscene. The filthier the better, in fact. It makes our job easier. And you needn't look."

Dr Grainger smiled at Nurse Almond, Nurse Almond wished that Dr Grainger would drop dead, and Baker, who was so swollen by food that he was almost unconscious, adorned his canvas with three dung-coloured stripes. Nurse Almond looked hard and long, but she had to admit that she was disappointed. Nothing really obscene ever happened to her. Of course it might be an excellent dirty joke if you were well up in abstract painting, but to Nurse Almond it was just three stripes.

The day dragged slowly to its bloated close. Baker was sick in the middle of the group therapy, and then, after a large tea, he lay moaning on his bed, revolted by the great weight of slow digestion that he carried wherever he went, until it was time for supper. He had to be forcibly fed.

That night he slept the uneasy sleep of the overfed and over-tired, a sickly sleep disturbed by heavy dreams of midnight orgies in hot, walled gardens, where fat nudes of the late Venetian school sat indolently on fronds, with the moon shining soft on their bosoms, while in the centre of the garden stood a great statue of Queen Victoria, stark naked, ploughing through a mound of cottage pie.

The dawn came, and he awoke. As consciousness returned he felt his soul struggling to keep its mouth above a sea of food, and once again he was sick. He longed to be free. He longed for sympathy, for love and understanding. He longed for a mother.

The nearest to a mother that he would get that day was Dr

138

Grainger, and so he spoke to him. He knew that this was what they wanted, but never mind, he had suffered enough. He told it all. His hopes, his fears, his disappointments, the panacea, everything. He spoke of his youth, of his landladies, and of all the places where he'd lived. He told of his jobs, and he told too of Mrs Pollard, and of Miss Daisy Wilkinson, when he'd been Lewis, long ago. He told his story simply and concisely, with no dishonesty, and he enjoyed it so much that for a while his spirits rose. At first Dr Grainger was too busy congratulating himself on the tact and skill with which he was eliciting the information by remaining unobtrusive to catch more than the general trend, but such was the force of Baker's honesty that by the end he was listening with interest.

When it was over, when the web of truth had been spun and Baker had fallen out of the end of his life with a bump and was back in the mental home, there was a silence. Dr Grainger was thinking of all the things that he had heard, and above all of the two things that had not yet been revealed – who was persecuting him and what he felt guilty about. Baker was waiting for love and understanding.

"Somebody's been ruining your search, haven't they?" said Dr Grainger in something suspiciously similar to baby talk.

"Who?"

"You tell me. I'm here to help you."

Oh, if only that were true.

"Tell me who lost you those jobs. Tell me who's getting at you."

Baker looked puzzled.

"You won't feel so bad if you tell me about it."

"I've told you."

"You must trust me."

He did. He trusted this man.

"We can help you. We can help you to go about it the right way. We can help you find that panacea."

He hardly dared to hope that it was true.

"You've led a pretty aimless life. Wandering from place to place. No home. No career. Heaven knows, Baker, I yield to no-one in my desire for a better world. No-one yields to anyone in that. But I do it through my work."

"I've tried jobs."

"Not jobs. A job. I was lucky. I admit it. It's in the blood. We're all psychoanalysts, in our family. Dad lost his life doing it. He was pinned to the floor by a couch in Budleigh Salterton. I was in the canteen when they broke the news. Do you know what I did? I went out and did a group therapy."

A tear rolled down Baker's cheek.

"It's not always easy. I know that. Parents dead, unhappy childhood, poverty, bad breath. Problems of one kind and another. But you have to choose something. You can't expect to find the panacea except through a career."

Baker began to sob.

"You'll be quite safe here. They can't get you here. No-one can get at you here. We'll make you strong again. You're in good hands."

Baker began to shake.

"We'll cure you, and then they'll fix you up with a nice job."

Baker's shaking grew more violent.

"That's right. Have a good cry. Get it off your chest."

Baker's shoulders began to heave as the shaking took a grip on him. Dr Grainger summoned an attendant, who led him back to his room, shaking and gasping as the agony swept him away.

27

"SO WE STILL DON'T KNOW WHY HE THINKS HE'S BEING persecuted?"

"No, sir."

"It's paranoia all right, though."

"Yes."

"Three dung coloured stripes. That puzzles me. Why stripes?"

"No mention of it in Prude, sir?" asked Dr Grainger, referring colloquially to that well-thumbed volume, *The Social Meaning Of Colour – Babylon to Stevenage* by Virginia and Edgar Prude.

"No. It's disappointing. I was sure we were on the right track. The light blue seemed so obvious. The old school tie next, I thought, and back in the womb by Wednesday."

"The tie angle didn't produce anything, then?"

"No. We drew a blank. I had Harper check up. He even rang Gorringes. No school, not even in the colonies, has an old school tie with three dung coloured stripes. Never mind, Grainger. You've done your best."

"Thank you, sir."

"The fact remains that he feels he's being got at. It was obvious from the start. He felt we were getting at him. He felt we were prying."

"He has a strong sense of his own inadequacy."

"Yes. What do you make of this panacea thing?"

"He wants to be cured. He can't admit it to himself in personal terms – who can admit anything to themselves, in personal terms, without medical help? – so he persuades himself that it's the world that needs curing. A typical transferred reaction process."

"I think you're right."

"I know I'm right, sir."

"Well, the time has come to hand him over to Belling. See what he can do."

So Baker was sent to Wagon Twelve, where, along with all the other paranoiacs, he would be under the care of Dr Belling, a fearless Australian who had not lost his nerve even after being badly mauled by a patient in Goole the previous year. Dr Belling would cure him, if anyone could. It would have to be a rush job – only a month remained before they struck asylum and moved to Halifax – but he could do it if anyone could.

So Baker joined the three other paranoiacs under Dr Belling's care. None of them were serious cases – these were dealt with by the Goldplank or City Mental. They were three harmless, pleasant people whose lives would have been quite happy were they not being got at by, respectively, the Greek Government, the Methodists and the Old Bovinghonians Small Bore Rifle Club.

Dr Belling took the paranoiacs into the big tent each morning, and in the middle of the tent, in the treatment ring itself, he gave them certain objects – hoops, composition rubber balls to balance on their noses, tiny bicycles with square wheels, funny masks, all kinds of little objects that would help them to recapture their childhood and track down the source of their illnesses. Drugs, of course, also helped.

While he was exercised in that huge ring with its smell of wind and sawdust, and while he was interviewed in Dr Belling's room, with its faded photographs of grim little groups of long ago, each with its sad title, "Paranoiacs, 1957" or "Manic Depressives, 1949-1950", Baker was finding it extremely hard to accept that he was being persecuted. It was strange, admittedly, that everyone should be being got at except him, but surely he would have noticed if anything like that had been going on? And, anyway, who would do such a thing? The Greek Government? Surely not? The Methodists? What reason could they possibly have? And it couldn't be, it couldn't possibly be, the Old Bovinghonians Small Bore Rifle Club. No, he wasn't being persecuted. Life was bad enough without that.

But the idea stuck, as ideas will, especially when one has time on one's hands as Baker did during the long, lonely nights. He recalled those words of Dr Grainger, which had seemed so senseless at the time. "They can't get you here. No-one can get you here." Could it be that they were trying to make him believe that somebody was persecuting him, in order to avert suspicion from themselves? Was it they, his doctors, who were persecuting him? Ever since they had come into his life he had been questioned, imprisoned, harried. He began to read it in their faces. He realised suddenly how odd it was that he had been brought here so abruptly by Mr Lomax, and for no good reason. It was all a plot. They were persecuting him for some reason that he didn't understand, and they were trying to calm his suspicions and explain away his feelings of persecution by persuading him that he was a paranoiac. He, a paranoiac! Not in a month of Sundays. He, Baker, who had trusted so many people so implicitly all his life, and had so often been disappointed.

Disappointed, yes. Why had he been disappointed so often? Because they had all ganged up on him. All of them. He saw it all now. Ackroyd, Lomax, the Governor, all of them, all in the plot, all in league with the doctors, all softening him up ready for the moment when Dr Mildweed and his hatchet men could lock him up. All frightened men, frightened of what he might achieve, he and his panacea.

How few there had been on his side! Mrs Pollard, Mr Burbage . . . Mrs Pollard, where had she been when he was sent to prison? Where was she now? Why was she always absent when he needed her most? Where was Mrs Pollard when the light went out?

Surely not her? Not her. Not that kindly, loving . . . but then if she was a secret agent it would be her business to be kind and loving. Oh, it was clever. And to think that he'd never suspected a thing, never even noticed what a coincidence it was that it had been she who had answered the advertisement, of all the people who might have done so. How Dr Mildweed must have laughed as he'd told her what to say! He'd read of such things. People you trusted implicitly, and behind your back they sent coded messages to Moscow. Government officials were inveigled into making love with beautiful women who had tape-recorders wedged in both ears and a tiny camera lodged in their belly-button. Oh, Baker, how simple you've been.

It couldn't be true. The confidences they'd shared. The happy moments they had spent together. No, she hadn't sent coded messages . . . the letters! Mr and Mrs Elliott, and Mr and Mrs Lucas. What a fool he had been. What rings he'd allowed them to run. But the letters were his idea. Or were they? And even if they were, hadn't she planted the suggestion? That was enough. That was what these people did. They planted the suggestion.

But not Mr Burbage. Not nice old Burbage, helping him like that. Helping? A fine help he'd been. He'd still served a year in prison, for all that help. The sudden substitution for Ackroyd, on the day before the trial! And, then, when he came out, Mr Burbage waiting there. It was all so clear now. And he'd thought it was friendship. He'd soaked up the drink, made pacifist statements to that military poet, and then what had happened? He couldn't remember. Of course he couldn't remember. Somewhere, in the Ukraine, a roll of microfilm lay waiting to remind him. Oh Baker, Baker, Baker, your life was a mirage. Your friendships didn't exist. Those days by the kitchen range, lit by the flickering of a fire that had its birth in pre-history, they were a lie. That evening in the pub, allowing the warmth of friendship to spill over you, you were a laughing-stock. What have you ever shared? What has life offered to you, in all these years? Miss Daisy Wilkinson. That's all. Miss Daisy Wilkinson was the one person who was true, and Miss Daisy Wilkinson you rejected, long ago.

They came with drugs to kill him. He would not give them the satisfaction. He refused to eat the food that was provided, for fear that it was drugged. He knew what would happen if he ate it. First he'd feel drowsy, strangely drowsy, and then. . . .

Unfortunately all the food that arrived for Dr Belling's patients was drugged, the chef being the only Greek Methodist ever to cross the portals of the Old Bovinghonians Small Bore Rifle Club, so that if one wanted to remain undrugged one died of hunger. To starve was to play into their hands as surely as any other way, and quite soon Baker began to eat.

He found himself growing drowsy, strangely drowsy. Semi-conscious, he allowed himself to be swathed from head to foot in wet drying-up cloth. It was nice. It was relaxing. He lay in his big pram, waiting for his nice new Australian mother, and when she came he told her all his troubles.

In the semi-conscious days that followed his nice Australian mother learnt a lot about his patient. Clearly Baker believed himself to be unacceptable to society, and clearly this led him to see society – represented here by his doctors – as a hostile enemy ranged against himself. It was all so clear.

Under the influence of his treatment Baker grew more and more

144

sleepy, too sleepy to recall, in after years, what that treatment had been. He had been swept back, barely glancing at his childhood and adolescence, straight to the larval stage, back into the world's womb, where he was content to lie on his back and kick a little from time to time, in an effort to stretch his legs. He was living now in the misty, half twilight world of pre-history, enveloped in lethargy. He felt an immense desire for peace. He felt as if he had crossed a mountain range and had arrived at a place where it would be possible for him to lie undisturbed for ever under the warm sun, sheltered from the wind by a big stone, and to stretch his great legs to unbelievable lengths on the soft, springy grass. There he would be able to rest, as if Rip Van Winkle had remained awake to enjoy those hundred years of sleep.

But he was not allowed to rest undisturbed. Drugs were forced down him. People asked him questions and wrote down his answers in their books. Paint brushes and table tennis bats were thrust into his hands and he had to sleepwalk through a series of absurd exercises.

Then, after the drugs had been changed, little trickles began. The notes were taken with increasing eagerness. The energy grew stronger. Cooper grabbed a table tennis bat and was swiftly beaten 21-3, 21-2, 21-2. By that time he was exhausted, but later, as the hours passed, the energy took over again. Eventually, after a few days, his energy settled down to a nice, steady level and he was able to be taken off drugs altogether. He spent his time entering into all the rehabilitative exercises of the place – painting daffodils, playing table tennis, playing scrabble. A man of middle age, with little or no eye for colour, he had a poor sense of timing and lacked the clear head to see possibilities quickly, and his scrabble, table tennis and daffodils suffered as a result. But this merely meant that there was room to improve – and improve he would, of that he was determined.

The days were slipping past. Soon it would be time for the Mobile Mental Home to move on to Halifax. Each day a few more people were discharged, and the place was developing that air of forlorn festivity which comes when a routine is running to a stop.

Some of them felt better, some worse. Soon they would all be seeing their loved ones again.

But Cooper had no loved ones to see, and no home to which he could return. If he had a past, it had been wiped out. He knew the rules of scrabble and table tennis, and that was as far as his qualifications went. His competitive urge had been aroused at last, and it was through satisfying it that he would find true peace, but no man can satisfy his competitive urge with table tennis and scrabble alone. He needs more – much more. Cooper was determined to find it.

The day of his release dawned cold and snowy. He was half frightened and half stimulated by the challenge that he would face, and after finding himself unable to eat his breakfast he was taken to see Dr Mildweed. He joined a rapidly moving queue and after about twenty minutes found himself once more in the great man's caravan.

Dr Mildweed congratulated him on his recovery and presented him with a bill for £300. He asked for time to pay and Dr Mildweed made him sign an order promising to pay at the rate of £2 per week. "Perhaps that'll teach you to go sane in future," he said.

In the corridor, just as he was about to step out of the door, Cooper met Dr Grainger, who had come to say good-bye.

"Just off?" Dr Grainger asked.

"Yes."

"Have you any plans?"

"I'm going to get myself a job and find somewhere to live first."

"Good. Good. Well, the Ex-Lunatics Appointments Board exists to help people like you. Do you know where they are?"

"No, I don't."

"You'll find them very helpful. They're a great boon," said Dr Grainger, handing him a printed card with their address.

"Thank you."

"Well, I'm very glad to see you're so well. I wish you all the best of luck."

"Thank you."

Dr Grainger shook hands with surprising vigour. "And mind now," he said. "No relapses."

Cooper was somewhat surprised. He didn't recall ever having met the man before. But the advice was sound. No relapses. No, there would be no relapses. All that was over. He stepped out of the caravan, walked across to the gates of the Home, walked through Roundwood Park, white under its mantle of snow, and stepped out into the street.

He stood there, unable to decide which way to turn. He was cured. It was difficult to know what to do next.

28

"YOU'RE AT THE AWKWARD AGE," SAID THE DIRECTOR of the Ex-Lunatics Appointments Board. "Too old for the professions and too young for the school crossing patrols."

"I just want something steady and settled, sir."

"I know. I know. And if I could give it to you I would. If only you were younger there'd be a great demand for a Cambridge and Winchester Ex-Lunatic. You haven't filled in what previous work you've done, by the way."

"I don't know, sir."

"You've forgotten?"

"I'm afraid so."

"It's not your fault. It's the treatment. They've made you forget things. They've taken you back to your childhood. It's so selfish. I mean it may help them to know all about your tricycle accidents but one just can't expect it to interest the modern employer. He's too busy. Don't you know anyone who could tell us what experience you have?"

"I don't know, sir. I can't remember."

"Usually there's a close liaison with the next of kin, and we find out through them, surreptitiously. In your case no kin at all have put in an appearance. You've had no visitors. Frankly, Cooper, it's a difficult situation. I realise that there's a perfectly good medical reason for it, but it's bound to count against you. You go for an interview, they ask you whether you have previous experience of that kind of work, and you tell them you don't remember. It creates a bad impression. You see you may have the most tremendous qualifications."

"I don't feel qualified, sir."

"Well, you see, you wouldn't. You may have developed some fantastic specialised skill, of enormous commercial value, but how are we to find out, short of trying you at everything in turn? I mean if you'd been the Postmaster General I'd be none the wiser. It's not easy. Of course I can find you something but it won't be much. Or you could try the personal columns of the papers. There are always a few odd things where they might not enquire about your past. Odd's the operative word. 'Literary gent requires aide and confidante.' That kind of thing."

"I really want something quite ordinary, sir."

"Yes, I know. You're cured, and it's quite natural that you should. And also you'll have to build up your self-confidence. You want to start finding out your aptitudes. So perhaps it's as well to start with something humble." He began to hunt through his filing system and a ray of nervousness broke through the fog of Cooper's middle life. "Well," said the Director at length, looking up from his files and staring straight at Cooper, "There's only one thing I can suggest. It came in today. Commissionaire at the Royal Hotel. You're a bit on the young side – they like them sixty-five – but I fancy they might take to the idea of a graduate commissionaire. They're angling for their fourth star. I can't pretend it's ideal, Cooper, but it's money, and there is a canopy. You could wait and see for a bit, but I can't promise anything much better."

So Cooper became a Commissionaire at the Royal Hotel. He found lodgings near to his work, and attempted to settle down to his new life. He found it very difficult. It was hard to suffer the effects of a complete cure at his age. Here he was, a middle aged family man, a respectable citizen, and suddenly he was flung out into the world without an asset to his name. No family. No career. No qualification. No hobbies. He hadn't even any luggage. What use was a man without luggage? Somewhere there must be luggage, somewhere in the forgotten past of his there must be great trunks of the stuff, acquired in the course of twenty years of adult life. But where was it?

No luggage, so he had to buy things. Pyjamas, toothpaste, essentials of one kind and another, things he could ill afford. For he wasn't salaried, he was pittanced. He would have had trouble enough, trying to make ends meet, even without the two pounds he paid to Dr Mildweed, even without these essentials he had to buy. He wasn't a drinking man, so far as he knew, but he'd have liked to have a local, somewhere to pass the time of day with a few cronies. But how could he possibly enter a pub, a man with no means? And even if one day he began to have means, what would be the use unless he developed a past to go with them? How could he go into a pub, with no opinions? "What do you think of capital punishment?" "I forget." He'd be a laughing-stock.

Those long hours in his lodgings, when he wasn't at work, how dreary they were. He was too old to start having new interests, and he couldn't recall the old ones. So he sat there, living on bread and tins of soup, and searching desperately into his past.

The last thing he could remember was the arrivals platform at Liverpool Street Station. He got out of the train, and set off at slightly above normal pace, for he was eager to leave his youth behind and pass out into the world, where he would be able to . . . to what? What, what, what? He remembered only the eagerness with which he had set out, with a degree in his pocket and hope in his heart. And after that, nothing. Fog rolled in off Bethnal Green, an engine hooted, and he awoke in Dr Mildweed's Mobile Mental Home. It was no use. Try as he did, he could remember nothing in between. A youth, as clear as if it was yesterday. An early middle age, as vivid as if it would stretch to the end of time. And nothing in between.

If you're lonely in lodgings you live for your work. How could

Cooper live for his work? What a job. What a self-conscious farce, in his green uniform and hat, with "Royal Hotel" inscribed in braid letters. Anything else would be better than this. If only he had capital he could start up a small business, for when he married late in life the respectable widow who had begun to figure prominently in his dreams. Nothing great, he was too old for greatness. Old men did sometimes become great but they had begun working towards it when they were fourteen. Just a modest little business. Cooper Ltd. One day it might be Cooper and Son. Cooper, licensed for the sale of alcoholic liquors. Fruiterers and Cooper Greengrocers. If only he had the capital, and maybe he did, but where? And under the circumstances who would offer him a loan?

He felt quite incapable of continuing as a commissionaire. It wasn't the duties. These he could manage. Opening car doors, raising his hat, conjuring taxis out of traffic jams, pocketing tips without letting anyone see that you were fingering the coins to tell how much there was there – these were not totally beyond him. What he utterly failed to achieve was the manner that goes with them, that blend of massive authority, unassailable dignity and utter stupidity without which the porch of no four star hotel is complete.

Everyone looked at him. Everyone wondered what he'd been before, as if he didn't wonder enough about it himself. It was obvious that he'd been used to better things. What better things had men who'd been used to better things been used to before they became used to the worse things they were used to now? They'd been army officers, rendered superfluous in their forties, or champion boxers, too punch-drunk to hang on to their ill-gotten gains, or clergymen, men of bottomless high-mindedness defrocked for one isolated and unspeakable enormity. The patrons could see, and so could Cooper, that he was physically incapable of being an ex-boxer or a retired officer.

The thought that he might be a defrocked cleric weighed heavily on him. It was not only that he got few of the tips that he so badly needed – people are reluctant to tip a defrocked cleric, for fear of hurting the finer feelings which may still be present beneath the

150

vileness. It was also that it troubled him greatly, this enormity of his, this lapse, this dreadful thing that he had done and which had probably been so closely associated with his illness. He tried even harder to remember. He tensed himself sometimes in desperation till all his veins throbbed. He pressed in upon his head with his skin as if he hoped to squeeze the missing years out of the top of his head. But all that came were a few dribbling bits of childhood, therapeutically invaluable but completely useless socially. Indeed the most remarkable feature of them was that they seemed to contain no clue whatsoever towards his future bent in life.

It was after a few weeks that he began to feel yearnings. Misery he had felt. Boredom, frustration, loneliness, weariness, despair, these he had felt. But not yearnings. Now they came. He would long to be far off. He would long to be free of this canopy to which he was tethered, nibbling for tips. He longed to fly. He longed to be climbing the road to the moors, up to the granite tors and away to the great beyond. He longed for something that would be all around him, and would embrace him in its inexpressible atmosphere.

Perhaps Mrs Pollard had passed by many times, not recognising him in his uniform, and he had not had eyes to see. Certainly she passed by that evening, and he did see her. He recognised her, and was unable to breathe. He was hollow inside. He wanted to rush forward, but he did nothing. He watched her disappear among the crowds.

He walked boldly into the hotel, went to the little room where the uniforms were kept, and changed into his ordinary things. Then he walked out again, less boldly, not looking to right or left. Nobody stopped him, nobody shouted after him, but he walked the best part of a mile before he dared to look round.

He went into four pubs and drank a whisky in each, quite slowly, watching the faces, listening to the hum of conversation. And all the while his course took him nearer and nearer to the objective that he still had not consciously recalled – Trebisall Avenue.

There it was. The name sent a thrill through his nerves that made him gasp and turn away. For several minutes he gazed into the windows of Pantons, seeing nothing. Then he turned away from the windows and walked hurriedly up Trebisall Avenue. He walked up the drive of number 38. He stood there for a moment, delaying his knock, and then, without being aware of it, he had knocked. There was the sound of slow footsteps, and heavy breathing. A face flattened itself against the frosted glass, and the door was slowly opened. Mrs Pollard stood before him.

"Welcome home," she said.

29

"I'LL MAKE YOU A NICE STEW," SAID MRS POLLARD. "It'll cheer you up."

At the thought of another stew his depression deepened. It was the second week since his return, and already he was feeling depressed. He left her to her stew, and wandered back, for the first time, to the little room where he had lived when he arrived in the city. It was empty now. Its whole spirit was empty, for it was now a dusty and neglected irrelevance. It was cold in that room, and the sofa had developed an air of prim permanence which made it difficult to believe that it could ever have been converted into a bed each night.

He felt a stranger here. Returning to the house ten days ago he had not felt that. He had welcomed the old life again with open arms. He had embraced Mrs Pollard and all that she entailed with enthusiasm, and had rejoiced to find himself once again in the warm comfort of her range, and of her bed.

From the very first moment he had felt the shame welling up inside him, and he had promised himself that he would atone for it in endless love. He would love this woman who had remained faithful to him although she believed that he had walked out on her. For she had remained faithful. She had called on Mr Begg, it was true, in Woodland Close. She had called, in the hope that her loneliness might be assuaged. She had taken tea with Mr Begg, and had discussed his old friend Veal with Mr Begg, but she had not stayed. She would never be able to assuage her loneliness except in Trebisall Avenue.

He glanced round the room. It was not meant for habitation now. No further lodgers were expected. She had waited for him, in case he should return. And he had returned, and almost as he had crossed the threshold he had recalled that horrible moment when he had believed her to have conspired against him. And the shame had poured forth, for he knew that she had not.

And now he was depressed. He lit the gas fire and sat in front of it, but it could not dispel the dust or make the walls of that room any more cheerful. He sighed, and glanced at the Scottish glen. It was grim under its lowering sky, and its sole occupant, a cow, looked wet and stupid, but he would like to be there in that glen, tramping the heather. The ivory ospreys, between which there were still no books, were unfriendly looking birds, but he'd have loved to stand beside the still, deep lake and watch them catching fish in their powerful claws.

Now Mrs Pollard was making him another stew, and he would have to eat it. He couldn't hurt her feelings. He had never deliberately hurt anyone's feelings, and he couldn't start now. Already the smell of the stew was growing stronger, and as it did so Cooper began to grow heavier. His weight was enormous. His great body hung in folds all round him. He began to sink. He sank into a swamp, where it was dark and the mud sucked around his mouth and nose, frothing as if it was alive, spitting and sucking and popping as if it had a thousand mouths. It grew darker and darker, and he grew heavier and heavier. He was sinking fast. He forced himself to rise up, to raise his chest out of the mud. His hair and his body were tingling with sweat, and then he began to see a thin point of light deep down at the bottom of his eyes. It grew steadily brighter, bringing with it a physical lightness. Now he found that he could raise his legs, that he could move his arms, that he had the energy to climb out of the morass. It was the most joyous experience he had known – a warm and wonderful relief.

He went to the window. It was dark, and there were plenty of things to be seen. Between the lights of the houses on the hills he could see gardens filled with all manner of beautiful things – sunsets, birds, mountains, forests, pagodas, waves breaking on the shore, sands that were pocked where the worms had been, trees bending with an approaching storm.

He knew that he must go, and he went upstairs, and fetched from his suitcase the quarto sheets of writing paper, covered now in green stains. He fetched his H.B. pencil, covered now in green stains. He fetched his souvenir rubber, on which the letters E TO M suggested a section of the alphabet of utterly no significance whatsoever. And armed with these things he went downstairs, and as he made his way to the little room Mrs Pollard came out of her kitchen to ask him what he was doing. "Writing," he told her with thumping heart.

"In there?" she asked, looking towards the little room with disgust.

"Yes."

"Authors!"

He arranged the various writing utensils on the table in the little room, and he wrote on one of the sheets of writing paper : "Small Ad, by Cooper." As he wrote he was conscious of odours of stew coming from the kitchen, odours which were constantly changing in the strangest ways. But he cast them from his mind, and eventually, after a few false efforts, he managed to complete his small ad to his satisfaction.

"Middle-aged gentleman, quiet, good education, desires simple comfortable accommodation with meals," it ran.

All that was needed now was to find a market for it. In the morning he would go down to the Central Library, and there, in the admirably comprehensive periodicals section, he would study the small ads columns of various papers, until he found one which suited the style of his. He felt confident that if he studied his market his small ad would be accepted.

He was ready for his meal, and now he felt hungry. He heard the kitchen door open and suddenly he dreaded the arrival of Mrs Pollard upon a scene that was so complete without her. Poor Mrs Pollard, he thought.

"Well, I don't know," she said, standing at the door and looking down on him as if he was a naughty child. "Back in your own room, catching your death from the dust."

"I've finished now."

"I should think so too. At your age." She paused, embarrassed. "It's the stew. I was wondering if you could come and help me with it. It's not going well, and I wanted it to be especially nice tonight, with your being depressed," she said.

Cooper brushed the mud off his clothes and followed her.

30

LIGHT, PERSISTENT SNOW WAS FALLING ON THE morning of his departure. He got up early, washed, dressed, shaved, packed, and went into the kitchen. Mrs Pollard followed him down.

"You're early," she said.

"I may as well make an early start."

"Are you sure you won't stay? You haven't changed your mind?"

"No."

"Only sometimes people see things differently after a night's sleep."

"No. My mind is made up."

"Well, let it not be said that I let you go with an empty stomach." Her voice broke just a little, and when she turned away he knew that she was crying.

She had cried the previous day when he had told her, after the reply had come. His advertisement had been accepted by a newspaper in Stoke-on-Trent, and a Mrs Wills had replied. It had been very difficult to tell her, but he had managed it, and then he had felt very miserable indeed as she had cried. She had beseeched him, but not for long. She had asked him why, and had not accepted his explanations, but she had taken it well.

"I don't know why you don't say what's wrong," she said, handing him his breakfast.

"I told you. Nothing is. It didn't work out."

"It could. With time."

"I can't stay. It's not personal. I told you."

"It is with me."

"You know what I mean. I told you. I came and now I have to go."

"You didn't have to come."

"No, but I did."

"You don't have to go, then."

"I do."

"You've got to discover the universal panacea for all mankind."

"Yes."

"Panacea, my hat."

"Do you think it's easy for me? Do you think I like this situation?"

"It's easier than it is for me."

"Please."

"Give it one more try." She looked at him beseechingly, and he found himself compelled to return her gaze.

"No."

She busied herself about her things then, and he went to their room and fetched his suitcase.

"Well," he said, putting the case down on the kitchen floor and standing awkwardly beside it.

"I'll come and see you off."

"There's no need."

"I want to. I don't want you to go all at once."

He wanted to offer her some rent, in lieu of notice, but he knew that he couldn't. She'd be insulted. He'd have to feel guilty about that. Once or twice, as they walked in silence to the bus stop on

156

the main road, he thought that he would offer it, but he did not.

The bus took them rapidly towards the station.

"E. F. Hebblethwaite."

"What?"

"That shop."

"Yes. Nearly there."

Soon they were there. Soon they were on the platform, with no train in sight.

"It's not in yet."

"It isn't due."

"How long?"

"Twenty minutes."

"Perhaps it'll be late."

She slipped her hand unobtrusively into his, so that he could ignore it if he wished, and, so quietly that he was under no obligation to hear it, she said: "Stay."

Then, louder, she said: "It's cold."

"Would you like a cup of coffee?"

"No, thank you. Not unless you would."

"No. I'm all right."

"There may be a buffet on the train."

"Yes."

He led her round the corner, where a wall would protect her from the wind. They stood there awkwardly, hoping that the train would soon come, hoping that it would never come at all. Occasional flurries of snow drifted in under the platform canopy.

"Well, it's a change, seeing my gentlemen off," said Mrs Pollard. "It's been the hearse, as often as not."

Cooper made a sort of sympathetic noise.

"Poor Mr Veal. I miss him."

"You've been unlucky."

"I've had my share of fatalities."

He didn't ask her whether she would take other lodgers. They fell silent for a moment, each with their thoughts, and then the diesel came throbbing in.

"Well, I'd better get in," he said.

"Yes. You don't want to have to stand."

He held out his hand, and she said: "Haven't you even got a kiss for your poor old landlady?" He kissed her awkwardly but affectionately on the cheek, laying his cheek beside hers for a moment.

"That's better," she said hoarsely.

He found a corner seat, put his suitcase on the rack, and lowered the window.

"It's not very crowded," he said.

"Don't get anything in your eye."

"I'm all right."

"I'll miss you." A tear trickled down her cheek.

"Yes."

"Look after yourself."

"Yes."

A whistle blew.

"Take care."

"Yes."

"I think you're off."

"Yes."

"The whistle's gone."

"Yes."

"You're off."

The train began to move.

"Good-bye," he said.

"Good-bye."

"Look after yourself."

"Yes. Write to me."

"Yes."

"Promise?"

"All right."

But he never would. She was falling back now as the train gathered speed, but he felt compelled to wave and prolong the agony. He waved, she waved. He receded, she receded. He was just a speck, she was just a speck. It was over.

31

IT WAS USELESS TO TELL HIMSELF THAT HE WAS ONLY arriving at lodgings – and unknown lodgings at that. He was arriving at the beginning of life itself. As the bus wound its way through the shabby industrial streets he forgot the mistakes and miseries of the past. He thought only of the future, the great future that was before him. He was growing nervous, as he had known he would. The dryness in his throat was growing tighter.

Here he was, at this moment, at this very moment in time and space, old Cooper himself, on the threshold of a new life, in which he would discover the universal panacea for all mankind. He got the letter out of his pocket and read it for the third time, to make sure.

"Dear Sir," it ran. "I have an excellent, newly decorated room on a pleasant housing estate. £4 10s. only per week with full board. You would not know it was the Black Country. There is a community centre, affording a good outlet for your education. I am sure it will suit you. I enclose a photograph. Yours sincerely. Mrs Wills."

The photograph showed a middle-aged woman, with a rather tight, prim face.

"Bannockburn Avenue," said the conductor, and Cooper hastily dismounted.

It was cold in these residential streets, and the sky was heavy with snow, but despite the cold he walked slowly. Soon, all too soon, he found Bannockburn Avenue. Somewhere up there was number 23, and somewhere in number 23 was Mrs Wills, who had answered his advertisement.

He paused at the door of number 23, delaying his knock. He

was near to panic. Then, without being aware of it, he had knocked. There was the sound of brisk footsteps. A face peered out for a moment through the frosted glass, and then the door was opened. Mrs Wills stood before him.

"You'll be Mr Smith." she said.

9 780007 427888